The Encyclopedia Codes

David Crystal

Other than the members of David Crystal's family and office, the characters portrayed in this book are fictitious. Any similarity to real persons, living or dead, is coincidental and not intended by the author.

Cover design: Hilary Crystal

www.davidcrystal.com

1

I'm responsible for the final break-up of the Soviet Union.

I used to tell the story as a joke. It was the only way I could get the bizarre things that happened to me in the first days of 1992 off my chest, without getting into trouble with the Official Secrets Act.

I've not been allowed to tell what really happened, until now. Actually, I'm surprised I've had permission at all. But, come to think of it, it is over 25 years ago, and the political situation has altered out of all recognition. Anyway, the fact of the matter is that last week, out of the blue, I got a letter - a real letter, not an email - from a part of the Home Office I'm not allowed to identify. It said my case had been reviewed and I was no longer bound by my 1992 oath. If I do talk or write about it, I just have to change some identities, as the people who helped me stay alive still have to work undercover. In some countries the politics haven't changed that much, it seems.

But then, thinking back, I'm not sure I ever did know the real name of my main contact. Gideon Awthrop, he said it was. What sort of name is that! I'll stay with it.

2

I first told the joke on 7 February 1992, when I was giving one of the Friday evening discourses at the Royal Institution in London. Now that's an unconventional experience, for any lecturer. It's an evening full of tradition. The speaker is led into a room near the lecture hall, ten minutes before the talk is due to start, and locked in, to prevent any escape. Apparently, in the early days of these discourses - so the story goes - a speaker was so traumatized by the elite scientific audience awaiting him that he turned and fled.

There's no escape now. You sit, drumming your fingers, and wondering how far you dare exploit the drinks cabinet. Then the sergeant-at-arms unlocks the door a few seconds before the appointed moment, marches you down the corridor, and thrusts you into the lecture room as the clock strikes the hour. You begin without any introduction, and you have to finish exactly one hour later, as the clock strikes again.

What had happened to me the previous month was so unexpected and frightening that all I wanted to do was tell people about it, and I knew I couldn't. I'd kept it to myself at the time. If Hilary had found out about it, or the kids, there would have been a panic, and that wouldn't have helped. And if my editorial team had realized that our encyclopedia database had been hacked, and why, they'd probably all have resigned on the spot. That wouldn't have helped, either. There were still deadlines to be met, spies or no.

So there I was, in front of several hundred listeners, with a brief to talk about my encyclopedia project and the history of the genre. This is how it all started. In 1986 Cambridge University Press, along with the Edinburgh firm of W & R Chambers, had asked me to be general editor of their new joint venture - what would later be published as *The Cambridge Encyclopedia*. It was a huge project, and it involved me finding a team of contributors to write about all areas of knowledge - 350 of them, in the end. I turned my house into an editorial office, and appointed a small editorial team. I had to build an extension to fit everybody in.

Anyway, it all worked out, and the first edition appeared, only slightly later than planned, in 1990. The idea was to revise it yearly, so the editorial team stayed on, trying to keep up with everything that was going on in the crazy revolutionary political years of 1989 to 1991. I used to joke that they weren't good years to be editing an encyclopedia. The one thing editors don't like much is change, because it messes up their beautifully written entries. If only the world would stay the same for a while, their job would be so much easier!

I don't crack that joke any more. Not after my encounter with the guild that really didn't want the political world to change, and would go to any lengths to stop it happening.

My talk to the Royal Institution was called 'On editing a modern cyclop(a)edia'. The odd title was a bow to Ephraim Chambers, who established the genre in 1728, when he published his amazing two-volume *Cyclopaedia: Or, an Universal Dictionary of Arts and Sciences*. I put the *a* in brackets because my project used the modern spelling. I talked about his work, and then about later encyclopedias, such as the *Britannica*, and my own approach to the *Cambridge*, and then, as the content was getting a bit dry and academic, I thought to lighten the mood - and in the process lift a weight from my shoulders - by telling everyone in a jokey way how the Soviet Union came to an end, thanks to me. Nobody could possibly believe it, so I wouldn't get into trouble with the authorities, I thought. It went like this ... but why don't I just reprint exactly what I said that evening? I don't want you to think I'm making any of this up. Here's the text as it appeared in the *Royal Institution Proceedings* Volume 64 for 1992, with just the occasional stylistic change. I'll add a few remarks as I go along.

I'd been talking seriously about the need for editors to keep their encyclopedias up-to-date, and how they're always being overtaken by world events. I pointed out that the editorial deadline - the date when final copy has to be sent to the publisher - is one where there's very little flexibility. And I went on...

> Nothing short of an event of world-wide significance will alter it. But one thing is certain: a month, or a week, or a few days before this deadline, that event will take place.

I gave some examples from 1989 and 1990 to prove my point:

> My deadline for the first edition of the *Cambridge* was 15 November 1989. On November 9, the East Germans opened the Berlin Wall. The next day Todor Zhivkov of Bulgaria was deposed. We put the deadline back two weeks, to see what would happen. A fortnight later, the Communist Party leadership resigned in Czechoslovakia. We put the deadline back another fortnight!

And then we went to press, hoping that nothing else would happen to make the first edition seriously out of date as soon as it appeared. But a year later we were in an identical position, as the deadline for the first reprint of the *Cambridge* approached. I had agreed the end of October 1990 with the Press. And then look what happened.

> On October 3, the two Germanies unite - 700 consequential changes to be made, as all contemporary references to East and

> West Germany go. The deadline is put back to the end of November. On 28 November, Mrs Thatcher resigns, with the consequence that entries on Major, Howe, Hurd, Heseltine, and Baker have to be altered.

Once again, after a couple of all-night stints, we just make our deadline.

So you can imagine the state of mind I was in as we prepared, a year later, for the second updated reprint, the one scheduled to appear in July 1992. The Press had given me a deadline for all revised copy: end of October 1991. I had an ominous feeling we'd never make it. All through July, as we routinely added the latest sports wins and the like to the database, I had this sense of impending doom - a sort of anticipatory deja vu. And then ... this is how I wrote it up:

> On 19 August there is a coup in the Soviet Union. I prepare for the worst. A few days later, the status quo is restored. I breathe a sigh of editorial relief. But my sigh is premature. In September, the independence of the Baltic States is recognized. In October the KGB is abolished. We postpone to the end of November.
>
> On November 4, almost all Soviet Union Ministries are abolished. The Soviet Union is fragmenting. I see over 1,000 references to the USSR falling around me like autumn

leaves. For a brief moment, there is optimism: on November 14, agreement is announced that the USSR will be replaced by a Union of Sovereign States - editorially, a superb decision, as USSR to USS will mean a change of only one letter. But a week is a long time in encyclopedia editing.On November 23, seven republics refuse to initial the treaty.

Will there be a change of name? I try to find out, and telephone the Soviet embassy in London to ask what they intend to call the USSR, both in English and in Russian. I am asked if I want a visa. I repeat my question. I'm told that it is the Western press which has published the new name (USS), not the Soviets, and that I should phone the Novesti Press Agency. Novesti does not know what the name is either, but think that if we must go into print perhaps 'ex-USSR' will do? The man who spoke to me cannot help with the Russian spelling, as he does not speak Russian, and in any case the Agency is closing at the end of the month. He gives me the number of the Society for Cultural Relations with the USSR. They are not answering the phone.

I call the Foreign and Commonwealth Office. The spokesman advises me to continue using USSR until the end of the year. There will definitely be no change of name before Christmas. A week later, the Commonwealth of Independent States is proposed, and on 20 December Soviet embassies all over the world are told to strike the name 'Soviet Union' from their records. So much for British intelligence.

My deadline is now 1 January. It cannot be held up any further, as the book is due out in six months. I have a busy Christmas eliminating 1000 references to the USSR. But dare I write an entry informing the readership of the reprinted *Cambridge* in July 1992 that there exists an organization called the Commonwealth of Independent States? Dare I write such an entry under letter C? I dare.

That's how I told the story to the audience at the Royal Institution in February 1992. It went down very well, judging by the smiles and the occasional laugh. It was, after all, a story hot off the press, for the new edition had not yet appeared. They didn't know what I knew, that just a few weeks before, this had been no laughing matter.

3

The courier from the Press arrived by motor-bike at 8 o'clock in the morning on the 31 December. Two of us had stayed up all night getting the last bits of copy in place. I'd left it until the very last minute to write my entry on the Commonwealth of Independent States. It was short, the bare bones:

> A body comprising 11 of the republics of the former Soviet Union, established after the dissolution of the Soviet state in December 1991. Georgia did not join the Commonwealth (*Sodruzhestvo*) because of continuing civil unrest. >> Armenia; Azerbaijan; Byelorussia; Georgia (republic); Kazakhstan; Kirghizia; Moldova; Russia; Tadzhikistan; Turkmenia; Ukraine; Uzbekistan

I attached the new entry to the relevant page of letter C, with a prominent red sticker to alert the printer that this was more than just a minor change and should be done first. Five extra lines would have to be somehow crowbarred into an already full page. I might have to lose some text somewhere else on the page to make up for it, so the sooner the entry was added, the better.

The courier put the large parcel of text into his pannier, and roared off. It would be in Cambridge later that day. I went straight to bed, had vivid dreams about monster typos, and woke in time to watch the New Year in.

Compared with the hectic December, Wednesday 1 January 1992 was an oasis of calm. Where we lived, it was mild, unusually windless, quite misty. We could hear the foghorn at North Stack grunting its basso profundo warning every minute or so. The house was strangely quiet. Lucy and Ben were both out with their friends. Nobody would be back in the office until the 2nd, and there would certainly be nobody working at the Press, so we weren't expecting any calls. Which is why, when the phone did ring, in the early evening, it gave us a start.

Hilary answered it, as she always does, but after a few seconds she put the phone down and called me over.

'It's someone called Gideon Awthrop - at least, that's what I think he said - from the Printing House. He says he's sorry to phone, but he must talk to you. Something about the new edition.'

'Can't you deal with it?'

'It has to be you, he says.'

I thought the worst. The courier had had an accident. There'd been a fire at the Press. All the marking-up would have to be done again. ... I took the phone from Hilary. 'This is David Crystal', I said, trying to sound nonchalant.

'I'm really sorry to call you like this but something's come up and I urgently need your help.'

All I could think about were my scrupulously marked-up pages.

'Has something happened to the proofs? Did they arrive OK?'

The voice seemed taken aback that I should ask.

'Oh yes, yes, they got here yesterday. But I need to talk to you about the next edition.'

'Go ahead.'

'Not over the phone. Will you be at home tomorrow?'

'Of course.'

'I'll be with you in the morning, then.'

'Well that's fine Mr Aw- '

'Gideon, please. And David, please don't tell anyone else about this call.'

'Why -?'

'I'll explain tomorrow. And one other thing.'

'Yes?'

'If you get another call from someone suggesting a meeting, ignore it. Or at least, don't agree to anything until I've had a chance to talk to you.'

'All right. But what's this all about? Can you give me a clue, in case I need to prepare something?'

'There's nothing to prepare, I assure you.'

'Well ...' - I concluded weakly - 'See you tomorrow, then.'

'Ten o'clock OK?'

'Fine.'

And he rang off. I gave the phone back to Hilary, who was looking as puzzled as I felt.

'What on earth was that all about?'

'I've no idea'.

I told her what Gideon had said. She thought for a moment.

'It must be something to do with the entries. Do you remember the time when we got a postcard campaign complaining about the way one of our entries had been written?'

I certainly did. It had been an argument over what to call a famous stretch of water in the Middle East. Should it be the Persian Gulf, or the Arabian Gulf? Or just the Gulf? My policy was to follow the directive of the United Nations. But that didn't satisfy some people, who thought that if they flooded us with postcards we would change the name to suit their cause. Today we'd be flooded with emails. But this was 1992. No emails then.

'Maybe something like that has come up in the Press, and they want to advise us about how to deal with it. Perhaps this Gideon is from their legal department, which is why he's being so cagey.'

'He didn't tell me which department he was from. No, wait a minute - didn't you say he was from the Printing House, when you answered the phone?'

'I did. I'd forgotten that.'

'Well he's unlikely to be from the legal department, then, as they're in a different building altogether.'

We lapsed into a thoughtful silence.

'Maybe the book has been put up for some sort of prize, and it's all secret...?'

'Ever the optimist, Hilary!'

We tried out several other scenarios on each other, dismissing each one in turn, until we ran out of ideas. Then the previous day's overnight stint caught up with us again, and we went to bed early, leaving a note for the kids: last one in, lock the front door. We slept right through. It would be the last time for me for a while.

4

Gideon arrived at ten, on the dot. It had been a busy morning. The editorial team had come back after the break and were settling down to the routine. Checking the New Year's Honours list for changes to be added to biographies, that sort of thing. I assumed he'd want to meet everyone in the editorial office, upstairs at the back of the house. That's what previous Press visitors had always done. But he declined.

'I don't want anyone else to hear what we're talking about.'

He walked briskly into the sitting room, carrying a travel suitcase, and looked around, as if he was surveying it for a house purchaser.

'This'll be fine.'

We sat opposite each other by the long picture window. Athletic-looking chap. Well-built. Early forties, I supposed. A fringe of fair hair flopping down over what seemed to be some sort of scar, or birthmark, on his forehead. Went straight through his eyebrow. I'd been to the Press several times, and I'd definitely never met him before. I wouldn't have forgotten a face like that.

Hilary had made us a jug of coffee. He sipped away as he took in the view.

'Nice.'

Did he mean the coffee or the view? I smiled in a way that I hoped could mean either.

'What's the hill called?'

'It's a mountain, actually. Holyhead Mountain.'

A laconic grunt.

'Mynydd y twr. ... In Welsh.'

Another grunt.

'There's an old Roman watchtower at the top. And some Iron Age hut circles on the lower slopes. You can't see anything today, though.'

Silence.

The top of the mountain was still shrouded in morning mist. It's got its hat on, my mother used to say. In the garden, two seagulls were fighting angrily with each other over a piece of bread. I was wondering just how much more tourist chat I could come up with, when Gideon put his cup down on the table, opened his case, and took out what looked like a page from a passport.

'This is my ID.'

'Why do I need to see your ID?' I knew Cambridge University Press were safety conscious, but this seemed a bit excessive.

'Because it shows I'm from -' and he named an agency of the government Security Service that I reported in the first draft of this story, but was deleted by the censor who cleared this book for print.

'You're not from the Printing House, then.'

'Well I am attached to the Printing House, sort of, for the time being.'

He got out another sheet.

'And can I ask you to sign this before we begin.'

'What is it?'

I looked at the page. MOD Form 134. Official Secrets Act and Confidentiality Declaration. I'd never seen such a document before. I'd heard of people 'signing the Official Secrets Act', but had never been entirely sure what that involved. Now I could see for myself. I scanned down the formidable set of obligations.

> I am aware of the Official Secrets Acts and that I am subject to them and that there are serious consequences if I am found to be in breach of them.
>
> I understand that I have a Duty of Confidentiality to the Ministry of Defence and that I may be in breach of that duty and of Crown copyright if I disclose any official information without prior permission of the Ministry of Defence.
>
> I understand that where I gain access to or am entrusted with official information, in whatever form and by whatever means, it is my duty to continue to protect that information.

And several more. I looked up at Gideon, who had a pen at the ready. I signed it.

'Right, now we can get down to business.'

He folded my declaration and put it carefully into his case.

'This all started a few months ago, when we noticed an abnormal pattern of behaviour in the way your encyclopedia was being sold abroad, especially in territories belonging to the Soviet Union.'

'The former Soviet Union', I interposed.

'Indeed. But that's to anticipate the issue we're going to be talking about. You'll be familiar with the spy ring that operated from Cambridge some time ago.'

'Of course.' I'd edited the entries myself. The names had become part of espionage folklore: Guy Burgess, Donald McLean, Kim Philby, Anthony Blunt, and a couple of others whose names I'd forgotten. It all happened in the 1950s, when the Cold War was at its height.

'I have them all in the encyclopedia. But that was nearly half a century ago.'

'A short time when it comes to espionage forward planning. The story was put out that the network was broken, and everyone had been identified. And indeed the main players had. But there was one member of the ring we left in situ, as it were.'

'Ah, a rotten apple.'

'Excuse me?'

'There's a rotten apple, Jim.'

'I don't get you.'

'Don't you read John Le Carré?'

'I don't read spy stories. Too much like work.'

'Well I do. This is *Tinker, Tailor, Soldier, Spy*. George Smiley talking to Jim Prideaux, and telling him about the mole in British intelligence.'

I couldn't tell whether Gideon was impressed or not. He carried on.

'We knew who he was, and where he worked, and our thought was that it would be useful to leave him there, keeping a close eye on him, of course, on the assumption that one day the Soviets would reactivate him.'

'And they have?'

'In May 1990, this man applied to the Russian Embassy for a holiday visa. It was granted, exceptionally quickly, and he was away for a week. Our people tailed him to a hotel in a small town not far from Moscow, where he met a group of others. They spent the whole day holed up there, planning we don't know what. But our man took photos of everyone as they left, and we've been able to identify them.'

He pulled out a sheet with eleven photographs on it.

'The names won't mean anything to you, but their countries of origin will.'

I looked at the caption beneath each picture. Armenia, Azerbaijan, Byelorussia, Georgia ... I looked at Gideon.

'Why, these are all the states of the Soviet Union. There's one from each.'

Gideon nodded.

'And each one is very highly placed. This was a powerful group. And the fact that they met within days of the Soviet coup on August 19th we think is significant.'

'The short-lived coup.'

'As far as we know. From the outside things are never what they seem, especially in the USSR. The question is: what are they up to? From our other sources we know there's a powerful group being formed that wants to overthrow the new regimes and restore the Soviet Union. There's a lot of grass roots support for the old system, you know.'

I didn't know. I had thought that everyone was in favour of political change - but not, it seemed, in the Eastern bloc.

'We know that at least three of the new leaders are being targeted for assassination. Could be more. Obviously to have greatest effect the whole plot would have to be coordinated. Imagine the impact: on a certain day, at a certain time, liberally minded politicians in all twelve countries are taken out. The old guard steps in. Bingo.'

It was at this point, I think, that I thought it was time to wake up and find out this was all a vivid dream brought on by late-night editing. I got up, walked to the window, stared at the mountain, blinked very hard three or four times, and turned back into the room. Gideon was still there. He looked sympathetic.

'I suppose this has come as a bit of a surprise.'

'You could say that.'

Then I remembered to ask the obvious question.

'Why are you telling me all this?"

'Because we think you may be able to help us find out what's going on.'

'Me!'

'You're in a unique position, as editor of the encyclopedia. You know that database better than anyone else.'

'But what's the encyclopedia got to do with it?'

Gideon took a paper out of his case, and checked off the points.

'This is our reading of what's happened so far. A year ago, the first edition of your encyclopedia is published. We keep a note of all foreign sales, especially to countries that are, so to say, sensitive. It was spotted that a single copy of the book went out to the Soviet embassies in each of the eleven satellite states. And one to Moscow, of course.'

'What's so strange about that? Surely book orders come in from all sorts of places all the time?'

'There was no record of any order. Somebody here decided to send them.'

'As a publicity campaign?'

'Hardly. It's reasonable to imagine the Press wanting to attract sales of an English-language encyclopedia in English-speaking countries, but not really in countries where hardly anyone speaks English, and where a book of this size would be well beyond what ordinary people could afford.'

'Go on.'

'A month after our man returns from Moscow, we intercept a mailing from Cambridge to all the embassies. Inside each letter is a piece of notepaper headed the Global Shakespeare Association, and a single word: 'tragedy'.'

'I've never heard of a Global Shakespeare Association.'

'There is no such organization - at least, not until this group was formed.'

'So it's some sort of Shakespeare club, then?'

Gideon looked mildly irritated.

'It's clearly some kind of front. As you'll see when you look at the words. A new word is sent out on the first of each month. Here's a photocopy of each one to the end of 1990. They're all entries in your encyclopedia, by the way.'

He dealt them out one by one on the table.

September 1990	tragedy A4B2F55
October 1990	comedy Z3W3
November 1990	sonnet I66J71Q8
December 1990	Stratford Y18L19D3
January 1991	Antony M2S7T61
Feburary 1991	Macbeth P1S3X141

March 1991 Othello R5S2V8

I wasn't impressed. 'Well of course they are,' I said. 'They're pretty basic notions. Seems innocent enough. Looks like some sort of game, or competition. Write a story beginning with the word. Kind of thing they do in school.'

Gideon took no notice, and carried on. 'But then we get this.'

April 1991 Latvia I23T07S10E04

'Perhaps you can tell me what the relationship is between Shakespeare and Latvia?'

I shook my head.

'Or what that string of characters means?'

Another shake.

'And why it just so happens that, five months later, in the morning of the 11th September, a group of twelve meets in the theatre at Ivanovo, near Moscow, apparently without any further communication taking place between them, other than these monthly letters?'

'And they carried on with just one word each time?'

'Here's the set for the rest of last year.'

May 1991	Lear P1Q1R36
June 1991	Verona B12D17
July 1991	Shrew M41N32J06
August 1991	Windsor S12D03T08
October 1991	Cymbeline V16G17P13

November 1991 Hamlet H45E14T14
December 1991 Venice M21N22

'Nothing for September.'

'No point. They met together that month. The question is: how did they know the place, date, and time? If our Cambridge man is the organizer, as he seems to be, how did he tell them?'

I stared at the list, blankly.

'We checked. One of the rooms at the theatre had been booked for the day by this Global Shakespeare Association.'

I felt I had to say something, and thought a Shakespearean quotation about plotting might be better than total silence, when Gideon added another photocopy to the pile.

'Then yesterday, we get this. Exactly one year later.'

January 1992 Belorussia +1
A05A05S08S30C24G02E19C31
B23B04L14T07H17E04F07

'Why the +1?'

'No idea. Nor why the string of characters is so long. But if the message has the same significance as Latvia had last year, it means they're getting ready for another meeting - and we want to be there. We need to know what they're planning. It has to be something big. The final details of the assassination plot, we think.

And it's got to be soon. Russia was accepted as a UN member just a couple of days ago. The other states are likely to have their UN membership ratified in the next month or so. If they;re going to do something, it has to be ahead of that.'

'So where do I come into this?'

'Well, you know the encyclopedia better than anyone else, so we were thinking that you might be able to see, well, some pattern in the messages.'

'You mean you think it's some sort of code.'

'Exactly.'

'But why come to me? Haven't you guys got codebreakers that do this sort of thing for a living?'

'Oh sure. But we worked on last year's messages and nothing came up. It's definitely not a cipher.'

He broke off. 'You're familiar with the difference between a code and a cipher?'

'Of course. Ciphers use letter substitutions. Codes use word substitutions. The term 'code' has evolved a wider meaning over the years, so that in everyday usage anything that is encrypted can be called a ... '

I tailed off. I had switched into lecturing mode. Gideon was already looking bored.

'.... code, yes. We had our people in Cheltenham work on it. They tried every cipher-breaking system we know, and nothing came up.

If it's anything, it has to be a word-based system, and that's where the problem lies.'

'I don't follow. Oh, no wait a minute - To interpret the code, you need a code-book.'

'Right. And that could be anything. It could be a book by Karl Marx, for all we know. Anything. As long as everyone has the same copy, they can work out how to translate the coded words in the message.'

'Judging by the words in your letters, it looks like it ought to be a copy of Shakespeare.'

'Yeah, but that's too obvious. That's like they'd be telling us: hello, this is the way to break our code? No way. And in any case, these are modern country names. They're not going to turn up in Shakespeare.'

'Certainly not Belorussia,' I muttered.

'What was that?'

'Oh, sorry. Not Belorussia.'

'Quite. If all these words are code words, the key is going to be found in a book that contains both the Shakespearean words and the country names. So...'

I had a light-bulb moment, and my words coincided with his.

'... the code book is the encyclopedia.'

5

'Any more coffee in that thing?'

Gideon pulled a copy of the encyclopedia out of his bag while I poured us both another cup.

'That's what we think, anyway.'

He flipped through the pages.

'It's a big book. How long did it take you to bring all this stuff together?'

'Three years, more or less.'

'And how many people were involved?'

'About 300, in all.'

'Specialist contributors?'

'Yeah. For instance, all my natural history entries were compiled by a team from the Natural History Museum in London. My space exploration entries came from someone at NASA. And so on.'

'Who did the Shakespeare entries?'

'A literature academic. There's a list at the back of the book.'

'Yeah, but it doesn't say who wrote what.'

'No, but I can tell you who's who, if it's important.'

'It might be.'

My brain was racing. Could any of my contributors possibly be a spy, writing coded entries? Absurd. Apart from anything else, all entries as they came in were edited by the members of my team, and then finally by me.

Quite often, the entry that ended up in the encyclopedia had lots of changes from the one that was sent in. Some of the specialists would write entries that were superbly accurate, but difficult for a general reader to understand. That was my job, as an editor: to rewrite them so that they were a comfortable read. If any of the entries *had* been carefully coded hy a contributor, there was no guarantee that they'd survive the editing process.

'And that applies to the gazetteer entries too,' I said out loud.

'Huh?'

Gideon wasn't keeping up, I thought. And then I realised I hadn't said any of my train of thought aloud. I'm always doing that. It's why professors are called absent-minded.

I explained my thinking, and added: 'The data about all the countries - their towns, physical features, and so on - that all came from a different source, a gazetteer that Chambers published a little while go.'

'Chambers?'

'Yes, the Edinburgh publishing house, W and R Chambers. They were in cahoots with Cambridge at the beginning of this project. The encyclopedia was going to be a co-production. But for various reasons Chambers withdrew.'

'Which is why it's now called the Cambridge Encyclopedia.'

I nodded.

'So the entries in your book are the same as those in the Chambers book?'

'Not exactly. They all had to be updated - latest populations, that sort of thing. And of course, the political events of the last couple of years have meant that several countries have had to be completely rewritten. New names, in many cases.'

Gideon flipped through some more pages. 'Which is where we started. Because all the people at my little meeting come from countries where there's a demand for independence, and with that usually comes a new name.'

'Sure. They won't want to be called a 'Soviet Socialist Republic' any more. And that's my main problem with this next reprint of the Encyclopedia, the one I just sent to the press. I don't know whether they're all going to stay with the names they have now, or whether they're going to group themselves into some new organization. I've had to make a guess.'

'A guess?'

'Well, an informed guess. I ask my politics contributor, the Foreign Office, sometimes an embassy... Getting rid of the USSR was the easy bit. Finding out what's going to replace it is a lot trickier.'

'What do you mean? Getting rid of the USSR?'

'I've spent the last couple of weeks deleting all the contemporary references to the USSR. You can see all the deletions marked in the proofs. There were over a thousand places where it had to go. It wasn't the most relaxing of Christmasses.'

'And the replacement?'

'Well, last month I heard that the new republics would join together into a Commonwealth of Independent States. I got that from the Foreign Office. So I've written an entry about it.'

'But it doesn't exist yet. It might never exist.'

'I know. A week is a long time in politics. Sure, anything could happen. But look at it from my point of view. If the CIS does get itself organized, and the new edition of the encyclopedia comes out in July, there's got to be an entry about it, or the book will seem horribly out of date as soon as it's out.'

'But if the CIS doesn't happen, and your book comes out containing such an entry, it'll seem horribly wrong.'

I grinned.

'Yes, I know. That's the excitement of being an encyclopedia editor. People think such a job must be terribly boring. It's anything but. You're always trying to keep up with life, and life is moving very fast, especially in Europe at the moment.'

'Can I see it?'

'It's in the marked-up proofs.'

'Yeah, but I haven't seen those yet.'

I went upstairs and printed out the entry. When I came down, Gideon was standing up and looking out of the window.

'What did you say that was called?'

The mist was lifting from the mountain.

'Holyhead Moutain. Mynydd y twr. Mountain of the tower, in Welsh.'

'Looks like a nice place to go walking. Or climbing?'

'Yes. There are some great climbing cliffs around the other side. The Everest team practised here in 1953. Over on the left - you can't see it from here - is South Stack, where the lighthouse is. Great tourist spot. But quite dangerous if you don't stick to the paths.'

Too much information. Gideon had already sat down.

'Let's see the entry.'

> **Commonwealth of Independent States**
> A body comprising 11 of the republics of the former Soviet Union, established after the dissolution of the Soviet state in December 1991. Georgia did not join the Commonwealth (*Sodruzhestvo*) because of continuing civil unrest. >> Armenia; Azerbaijan; Belorussia; Georgia (republic); Kazakhstan; Kirghizia; Moldova; Russia; Tadzhikistan; Turkmenia; Ukraine; Uzbekistan

'You can see,' I added, 'that I tried to have my cake and eat it. I've written it as a historical entry, which will be valid even if the CIS does collapse at some point.'

'You don't mention the three Baltic states.'

'I don't know what's happening there. I've tried to find out, but the Foreign Office doesn't seem to know either.'

Gideon rubbed his chin.

'Estonia, Latvia, and Lithuania won't want to join, as they see their membership of the USSR as something forced on them. They wouldn't want to be part of any new organization. In their view, the CIS would be simply the USSR under another name. But the interesting thing, from my point of view, is that the countries you do list are exactly those who came to the meeting in St Petersburg.'

'That's probably a coincidence.'

'I doubt it..'

Gideon thought for a moment.

'Do you know what I think? I think this entry will give our friend in Cambridge a bit of a shock. He thinks nobody knows of the membership of his Global Shakespeare Association, and now here's an entry that actually names the eleven members. It misses out the three that don't want to be there, and draws attention to the one case where there's a problem.'

'So?'

'My guess is that he'll think you're onto them. He'll work it out like this. It would be crazy to write an entry for something that doesn't really exist yet. So if you do write one, it must be for some other reason. And the only other reason is that you want to let this Shakespeare group know that you're watching them.'

'Me?'

'Well, when I say you, I mean you in league with us. He'll assume that you're working with British intelligence.'

I laughed, weakly.

'Did you draw attention to the CIS entry?'

'I did. I wanted the printer to deal with it first. I put a big red sticker on it.'

Gideon's face was a picture. The caption: 'Well there you are, you see'.

'And, moreover, he'll assume you've cracked the code they're using, or are in the process of cracking it.'

'But I haven't. I mean, I didn't even know there might be a code until just now.
This is all very far-fetched, Gideon.'

'Not in the least. I'm trained to try to think like they do. Trust no-one. See plots everywhere.'

I looked out of the window. The mist had descended on the mountain again. Gideon went on.

'That's why I told you not to meet anyone until we talked. And if someone does try to get in touch from now on - someone unexpected, I mean, someone unusual - then let me know straight away.'

'Wh- why might that happen?'

Gideon stood up.

'Look, I don't want to scare you - '

'You've done that already.'

'- but if I were them, I'd want you out of the way. They think you know their code. They see evidence of this, as they think, in the CIS entry. Our man in Cambridge will have no trouble getting hold of your proofs and erasing all mention of the CIS. But he may just take it into his head to make sure you don't have the chance to tell what you know to us.'

'You mean - '

'A little accident, walking on those cliffs you told me about, perhaps. It's happened before. Whenever you read of a foreign diplomat dying because of a car accident or a disease or whatever, there's usually something more to it. It happens to us as well as them. It's the game we're all playing.'

'And now this is the encylopedia game.'

Gideon smiled.

'Precisely.'

'Gideon, I have to say, I don't want to play.'

He leaned forward.

'It's too late for that, David. Whether you like it or not, you're in. You don't have a choice. And my job is to ensure that you stay safe and well, so that you can edit more encyclopedias.'

He looked again at the mountain, and waited.

I suppose half a minute went by before I said, 'So what do I have to do?'

'That's easy. Find that code and crack it.'

6

Gideon left soon after, telling me he wasn't going far. He'd booked in to a nearby B&B, and would stay there, he assured me, until things became clearer, whatever that meant. He gave me the phone number of his mobile - the latest Motorola model, I noticed. Also, he added, I might need some help, and he'd be able to get it for me. I wasn't sure what that meant either.

Hilary joined me after he'd left.

'Useful meeting?'

'Very.'

I tried to make myself sound as nonchalant as possible, and totally failed. She looked at me oddly.

'Is there a problem?'

It was a time for really fast creative make-believe.

'Not really. It's just that he's left me with a challenge, to do with - with marketing. Gideon's from the marketing side of the press, and they want to do something really different for the next reprint, so he's asked me to come up with some intriguing questions and answers for a quiz.'

Hilary seemed convinced. I warmed to my newfound theme.

'And I've got to do this really quickly, over the next few days, to meet their schedule.

They should really have got on with this before Christmas.'

'Will you need any help, from me or the team?'

'Oh no, no. I don't want you all to stop doing what you're doing. We can't delay the editing programme just because some guys in marketing have come up with a bright idea.'

She nodded, and we went into the kitchen to have lunch - or breakfast, in the case of the kids, who had just got up. I breathed a sigh of relief. After lunch I took myself off into a corner of the sitting room, away from everyone else, with a copy of the encyclopedia.

And stared at it.

And stared at it.

It was indeed, as Gideon had said, a Big Book. 1500 pages. 30,000 entries. 2 million words. If there was a code in there it could be anywhere. Where on earth to start looking? I tried to imagine myself as the Cambridge mole, planning the whole thing. If I wanted everyone to meet up, I'd have to specify a place, date, and time. And it would have to be completely unambiguous. 'Meet in the lounge of the Manchester airport Hilton at 12 o'clock on June 1st'. That sort of thing. At least a dozen words.

But how to get from the words in the messages to that end-point? I looked at the photocopies Gideon had left. Tragedy, comedy, sonnet, Stratford, words from the titles of plays, and then Latvia. Just one word in each letter.

Gideon's department had scanned all the letters for hidden messages, he'd told me, but there was nothing. So it had to be something to do with the words themselves.

I wasn't able to think about it properly until the evening. During the afternoon Lucy came in with some travel issues - she was going back to university in Edinburgh shortly, and we had to work out the best way of getting her there. I put Gideon's papers out of sight, and started to investigate a different kind of code - train timetables. Then Ben came in wanting to discuss the relative merits of the Commodore 64 and the new Nintendo and Sega entertainment systems. He had some Christmas money burning a hole in his pocket. Matthew wants to borrow my Dungeon Master, is that OK? Would Teenage Mutant Hero Turtles be a better buy than Super Space Invaders? Such things take time to decide.

I spent the evening in the study, after my team had left. The kids were downstairs watching Top of the Pops. 'Right, said Fred' ... 'Bohemian Rhapsody' ...

I looked again at the words in Gideon's list, getting increasingly depressed. There aren't that many ways of hiding words within words, after all, but I quickly realized that the old-style puzzles, such as anagrams and acronyms, weren't going to be of any use, because there was no way of knowing which words the guy in Cambridge had chosen for his message. The words in the letters were the obvious first place to look. T for tragedy, C for comedy... I'd put the first five up on my computer screen when Hilary came into the study. She looked over my shoulder.

'What on earth is TCSSA?'

'It's the first letters of some words, to see if they make an interesting anagram.'

She peered at them. 'No, they won't. CASTS and SCATS is all you get.'

I'd forgotten she did crossword puzzles a lot. 'What about LATVIA?'

'Nothing, other than nonsense. A VITAL. That sort of thing.'

I was grasping at straws. 'ARMENIA?'

'That's more like it. Nice balance of vowels and consonants.' She thought for a second. 'I AM NEAR?'

I wasn't, I thought.

'A MARINE?'

I shook my head.

'MAIN ERA? REMAIN?'

This wasn't getting me anywhere. I tried one more, without much hope. 'STRATFORD?'

'SORT DRAFT?'

She could see from my face I wasn't impressed, and I could see from hers that she felt doing something else - anything at all - would make for a more productive evening. She left me to it.

But crossword puzzles... Maybe, I thought, it would make more sense to work the other way around. I'd already got the answer to the question, after all. The meeting was held in the Ivanovo theatre on 11th September. The clues, whatever they were, had to lead to that solution. So if I started with those names, perhaps I could work out the clues backwards? I could ask Tony my techie to write me a program that would do the job, when he came in after the holiday. But the magnitude of the task was obvious. There would be just too many anagram possibilities. No... anagrams weren't the way.

I was getting tired. It had been, to say the least, a most unusual day, and I was still trying to make sense of it all. I joined the family to watch an episode of Last of the Summer Wine. Then the 9 o'clock news. Severe windstorm still causing problems in northern Scotland ... something to do with Latvia ... people still talking about Dirk Bogarde being knighted in the New Year's Honours list ... why Latvia, in the middle of all the Shakespeare words? Shakespeare never mentions Latvia... or does he? I felt uncomfortable. Better check.

I went up the the study and heaved down a Shakespeare concordance. The strains of Bohemian Rhapsody came from Lucy's bedroom. Everyone seemed to be singing it. Is this the real life? Is this just fantasy? Nope. No Latvia. ... Caught in a landslide, no escape from reality ... And then, out of curiosity, I looked up the other country names. ... Open your eyes... Russia turns up several times. ... Look up to the skies, and see ... And, surprisingly, Armenia. Twice. In 'Antony and Cleopatra' Caesar tells how Antony made one of his sons king of Armenia, and a few lines later says he will insist on a power-share in that country. Power-sharing... That seemed like a promising line. At least the context was political. 'For what I have conquered', says Caesar, 'I grant him part; but then in his Armenia, And other of his conquered kingdoms, I demand the like'. ... Easy come, easy go ...

Conquered kingdoms. That sounded like the Soviet Union - the *former* Soviet Union, I reminded myself, since Christmas Day. ... We will not let you go ... But I couldn't see a parallel between Caesar and Gorbachev, or anything in Caesar's speech that could possibly get me to Ivanovo. And anyway, the messages hadn't mentioned Armenia.

I needed to stay focused. Bohemian Rhapsody was reaching a climax. ... Mamma mia, let me - ... I shut the door, picked up a copy of the encyclopedia, and looked up Latvia.

> **Latvian SSR**, Russ **Latviskaya** or **Latviya SSR** pop (1983) 2 569 000; area 63 700 sq km / 24 600 sq ml. Constituent republic in NW European USSR, bounded W and NW by the Baltic Sea; flat, glaciated region; NW coast indented by the Gulf of Riga; chief river, the Daugava; over 40% forested; incorporated into Russia, 1721; independent state, 1918; proclaimed a Soviet Socialist Republic, 1940; occupied by Germany in World War 2; growth of a new nationalist movement in the 1980s;

independence talks with USSR, 1990; well-developed national folklore, particularly in the 1860s when the Latvian theatre was founded in Riga (1868); capital, Riga; chief towns Daugavpils, Liepaja; machines, metalworking, instruments, electrical engineering, electronics, chemicals, furniture, knitwear, food processing, fishing; cattle, pigs, oats, barley, rye, potatoes, flax. >> Baltic languages; Soviet Union

A completely normal, factual, uninspiring entry. No mention of Ivanovo, or anything related to it. No reason to. I looked up Ivanovo. It wasn't even in, as a separate entry. Too small.

Hilary came into the room, carrying a copy of the encyclopedia.

'You left this downstairs'.

'Oh thanks - I -' I stopped. I already had a copy of the encylopedia in my hands. And here was another one. Then it dawned on me. One was the first printing. The other was the second. In those pre-Internet days, it was essential to keep an encyclopedia up-to-date by repeated printings, so that new developments coud be added. The book had first been published in the middle of 1990, but all the dramatic events of that year had meant that Cambridge wanted a fresh printing in 1991 - and there was another to be published in 1992, which was the one I'd just sent to the press. I opened the two volumes at Latvia and put them side by side. Had I altered the entry at all? Was Ivanovo added somewhere?

Of course I had - as I'd had to do for the other countries that were in the process of disentangling themselves from the Soviet Union. Some of them had already announced their intention to be independent, and Latvia was one, so I'd added 'independence talks with USSR, 1990' to the entry. Everything else was the same. But it made me think. The mole must have sent out the first edition to his contacts. Did he send out the second printing as well? Had Gideon mentioned that? I couldn't remember. It might be important. I called his mobile.

'Huh?' A sleepy voice answered.

'David here'.

'Do you know what time it is?'

I didn't. I looked at my watch. It was almost midnight.

'Really sorry Gideon. But I just had a thought. Can you remind me. Did your man in Cambridge send out a copy of the encyclopedia this year as well as last year?'

There was a pause, and then a slightly irritated voice replied. 'Of course he did. I thought I told you that.'

'When?'

Another pause. 'Well, in July last year, when it came out.'

'So he sent out one copy of the encyclopedia in July 1990 and another in June 1991?'

'Yes.'

'Well... why?'

'Whaddaya mean, why?'

'Why bother to do that? It's virtually the same book. Just a few minor changes to keep it up to date.'

Silence. I went on. 'I mean, it's not as if - according to you - he's an educational philanthropist, and just wants to keep his friends happy by sending them the latest edition. There has to be some other reason.'

'Maybe...' - Gideon was clearly wide awake now - 'maybe he made some changes of his own. Changes you don't know about.'

'How would that be possible?'

'When is the last time you see the copy you prepare for a new edition?'

'When I send the final proofs off to the printer.'

'And that's, what, three or more months before the edition is published?'

'Yes.'

'So there'd be plenty of time for him to get hold of the proofs, and add an entry.'

'Well sure, but...'

'Worth a check, don't you think?'

It would be a big job, I thought, but I could get the editorial team onto it, and it wouldn't take more than a day. A simple job, though. All we'd have to do was compare the printed verson with the file in our database before it went off to the publisher, and -

'Get some sleep.'

We wished each other good night, though I doubt Gideon got very much sleep. No more did I. I spent much of it wondering how I would explain to my staff why they were having to carry out such a crazy task, when there was so much catching up to do after the Christmas break. Maybe I could say it was all part of a quiz... or a printer's audit... or ...

7

I realized I must have dozed off when the alarm shook me out of a vivid dream about running away, but with my feet sticking in some sort of mud that was slowing me down, and the thing behind me was getting nearer and nearer and - Eight o'clock. We had to open up the house to be ready for the editorial team, who would be arriving at nine. We had a very quick breakfast. I tried not to look preoccupied. I knew Hilary was sensing that something was up, but I hoped she'd put it down to the workload that we had to get through. Cambridge had told me they wanted to publish a concise edition of the big encyclopedia, as well as a factfinder and a biographical. A whole family of reference books. There was a huge amount of forward planning to do, and here was me saying to the four members of my team ...

'Before you carry on with what you were doing yesterday, there's just one small job to do...'

Faces fell. They'd been here before. My 'small jobs' would generally take them a week. But this time it really would be small, I reassured them.

'Tony will print off a copy of the database headwords, and all you have to do is check to see that each headword has turned up as expected in the book.'

'Why?'

I was expecting that. 'It's a check on the software the printer is using', I lied. 'There have been some reports that their program has been erratically inserting lines of text,' I lied on, 'and Cambridge want to check that it hasn't affected our headword list. The headwords should match perfectly, so if you spot anything that shouldn't be there, let me know.'

They seemed satisfied, as I divided up the alphabet into four roughly equal sections. A to G for Anne. H to L for Esther. M to R for Jan. S to Z for Hilary. That meant they would all finish at roughly the same time - around 2, I estimated.

I spent the morning trying to concentrate on something other than codes, but without much success. Normal things got in the way. A phone call. What had Gideon said ... someone unexpected? Hilary answered the phone. False alarm. It was for her. Then another. Why on earth was everyone ringing us up? First working day back, I suppose.

'It's for you.'

'What?'

'It's for you.'

'Who - who is it?'

'Someone from Radio 4.'

'Ah.'

I realized my mouth was dry, and I had - what was the phrase? - butterflies? Odd expression ... butterflies in the stomach ... must look it up, when it was first used...

'Well?'

'Oh, sorry. Ask them what it's about, would you? If it's for today, I can't do anything, I'm afraid. Nothing before next week.'

It was for today. Some politician had used an unusual idiom, and they wanted a comment. I wasn't in the mood for interviews.

It was 11 when Esther called me over to her desk. 'I think I've found one.'

My pulse rate shot up. 'Really? What is it?'

'Belo - how do you pronounce it? Look.'

It was Belorussia. This was promising. Belorussia was one of the countries in my CIS entry, and it was the latest mention in Gideon's list.

I looked at the page in the enyclopedia, and my pulse rate went back down. I recognized the entry. It was an extra cross reference that I'd added myself on the proofs. The entry began with the spelling B-E-L... but the new official name of the country name was Byelarus in English. Readers who looked it up at BYEL- wouldn't not find it, and they might not think to look under BEL-. So I had added a cross reference to help: Byelarus *see* Belorussia. Another false alarm.

And that's how the day continued. More nervy phone calls. And then the front doorbell rang. Hilary went downstairs to answer it. I hovered at the top of the stairs to see who it was, without her seeing me, and scuttled back to my desk before she came back up.

Only the postman. Something to be signed for. Nothing to do with me.

We broke for lunch. 'How's it going?' I asked the team. 'This is without doubt the most boring job we've ever had to do', said one. The others nodded. I smiled - I hope, sympathetically.

Two o'clock arrived. 'Finished,' called Esther. Nothing in H to L.

Half an hour later, Jan had finished M to R. Nothing.

Hilary was done by 3. S to Z. Nothing.

It was nearly 4 when Anne piped up. 'I've just finished G. I haven't found any extra headwords, but -.' She looked puzzled. 'I think there's one missing.'

'One missing?' I wasn't expecting that. Gideon had talked only about entries being added. 'Which one?'

'Gematria. Look.' She showed me the original headword list. There was the entry on gematria. She showed me the page of the encyclopedia.

She was right. There was no sign of the entry on gematria.

8

'What the hell's gematria?'

I'd phoned Gideon straight away. Nothing added anywhere, but in the entire encyclopedia just that one entry missing. I'd checked our database. There had definitely been an entry in the file we sent to Cambridge. I had it in front of me.

'It started out in the Middle Ages. It was a mystical way of interpreting words in the Old Testament of the Bible. Hebrew scholars would give numerical values to the letters in Hebrew words, add 'em up, and if some words had the same value they'd see this as very significant.'

'Like what?'

'Well I don't have any Hebrew examples in my head, but the method didn't stay with Hebrew. The idea caught on in other languages. And after a while it came to be used outside of its original religious setting. As a game, really - though some people placed great store by it.'

'You were going to give me a for instance?'

'Oh yeah, sorry. So, think of all the letters of the English alphabet, and give each of them a value from 1 to 26. A is 1, B is 2, and so on. Now... hang on a minute'.

I rummaged in my desk drawer.

'I've actually got some examples here from an after-dinner speech I gave the other week. Here's one. What sort of car will George H W Bush want to drive? Answer: a Ford Mustang. Why? Cos if you add up all the values of the letters in his name, they make 138. And that's the total of the letters in Ford Mustang. Get it?'

'That's crazy.'

'Sure... but it's fun. People love to hear of the unexpected links. Here's another. This one went down very well. JOHN MAJOR has the same total as BIG BROTHER - 104.'

Gideon laughed.

'You see? And also as MONSTER and DANGEROUS. You can go on and on.'

'But some people take these things seriously, you say.'

'Oh, deadly seriously. I even heard of a case where two people decided they should get married because their names added up to the same total.'

'Go on!'

'Really. Would you like me to do your name?'

'Sure.'

'It'll just take a second. Tony wrote a little program for me. Hold on. I have to put the phone down.'

I called up the program and typed GIDEON AWTHROP into the search box. 155. Then I typed that total into the box and looked at the list of results.

'Do you want the good news or the bad news?'

'Always the good news first.'

'Your total is 155. And so is KERMIT THE FROG.'

I heard an inarticulate splutter at the other end of the phone. 'And what's the bad news?'

'155 is also the total for SPYMASTERS.'

A silence.

'That's a bit near the bone, David.'

'You see, Gideon? That's how people get sucked into this kind of thing. Don't worry. It's just a coincidence.'

'But I'm beginning to think... maybe that's the sort of game these guys are playing.'

I took that in. 'Uh-huh'. I tried to sound non-committal.

'I mean, from what you've said, gematria is a sort of code - well, a cipher, technically. And that's the world we're trying to break into.'

Silence at both ends of the phone. Gideon spoke first.

'And it definitely couldn't have slipped through your net?'

I'd checked, before calling him. It was just possible I'd left gematria out myself, for space reasons, and it had slipped my memory. That sort of thing did happen. I'd had a similar problem in the Ys, for the new printing. Boris Yeltsin had come on the scene, and obviously needed an entry. I had to get him into the book somehow, but there was a problem. I'd been asked by the Press to keep changes to within a page. It would be hugely expensive if adding Yeltsin meant pushing other Y entries on to the next page. That's the domino effect. The next page would need to be reset, and then the one after... and so on until the end of letter Y. So I had to look around that Y page to see if I could make some cuts. Fortunately for me, the two Yemens - North and South - had merged into one, and the conflation would save me several lines. That's the sort of beautiful coincidence that editors pray for. But there was nothing like that on the gematria page.

'I don't think so.'

'Didn't you notice the omission when you went through the proofs?'

No, we hadn't. When proofs came in, we would give them a fresh read, as you would a novel. We'd only check statistical stuff against the database - population figures, and the like. The gematria entry had just been an ordinary piece of prose. If an entry was missing, we wouldn't have noticed. I made a mental note to do that kind of check in future.

I explained our procedure to Gideon. We both fell silent again. A longer pause, this time.

'You say you've got a program that works these things out for you?

'Yes.'

'For all the words in the language?

'Well, it would work for any word, but in fact I've used it only for the words in the encyclopedia. It was only for fun, remember.'

'Look, David.' Gideon' voice told me he had left fun far behind. 'I think we're onto something here. If you can make a cipher up like this so easily, then so could our man.'

'Well...'

'Let's assume he deliberately took out the gematria entry. Why would he do that? Obvious: to stop anyone in my line of work noticing it. Also, stupid. Very stupid. He never anticipated you doing the kind of check you did.'

'Yeah, but Gideon, listen... Even if he did do that, how could such a cipher possibly work?'

'Simple. You hide the real words behind other words that have the same value. Take Ivanovo. What's its total?'

I quickly typed it into my program. '98.'

'Right. Well he just finds another word with the same total and uses that instead. Same for all the other words in his message. All his contacts have to do is find the substitute words and look them up.'

'But to do that they'd have to have the same sort of program I've got here.'

'Sure - but that would be easy enough to share at their first meeting, when they set up the Global Shakespeare front. That's when he would've explained the whole thing. How long did Tony take to do the program.'

'I dunno. A few hours. He's good at that sort of thing. And he told me it wasn't a very complicated program.'

'So there we are, you see.'

It was beginning to sound the tiniest bit plausible, but several things were bugging me. A line from 'Antony and Cleopatra' flashed into my mind. A messenger is telling Cleopatra about Antony being friends with Caesar. Then he says 'But yet, madam -', and Cleopatra interrupts him: 'I do not like But yet'.

'Yeah, but - finding another word with the same total, 98. That's mad. There would be lots of words. How would he know which was the right one?'

'How many words have 98?'

I went back into my program. '960.'

'What are they?'

'Look, this is getting cumbersome. Come round, and I'll show you.'

He arrived at the front door ten minutes later, and we went up to the office. The editorial team had all gone home, so we were alone. Hilary was downstairs, I suppose a bit puzzled as to why the marketing man was still around. I'd concoct something to tell her later.

I showed Gideon the printout I'd made of all the words in the Encyclopedia with the 98 total.

'See what I mean? It's looking for a needle in a haystack.'

And indeed, it seemed so. There was Ivanovo, indeed, but surrounding it were nearly a thousand other words, in alphabetical order - abrasions, abridgement, accelerating ... all the way down to zealots, zloty, and zygote. Gideon scanned the list.

'There's no way a contact would be able to pick out Ivanovo from all that lot. There are too many other geographical names that could be meeting places. Even if we restrict it to the Soviet countries, there's Rybinsk and Tashkent as well. And if we go outside the Soviet Union there's Istanbul and Montreal ...'

'And Dunstable.'

'What?'

'And Heathrow.'

'Be serious, David.'

'Sorry. But you do have a point. There'd have to be some other clue. Maybe that's what the character strings are for?'

'I was just thinking the same thing.' Gideon got out his photocopies. 'Here's the Latvian one: I23T07S10E04. OK...' He got out a pencil. 'We divide it up into substrings.'

'Why?'

'It's a standard technique. I23, E04, T07, S10.'

'You could divide the string up in other ways.'

'Of course. But any code has to be based on patterns. It can't be random. And a string of three, with a letter and two numerals, is certainly a pattern.'

'So I23 might refer to the 23rd word under a list headed I.'

'Exactly.'

'Which might be Ivanovo.'

'Exactly.'

'But we don't know what the I refers to.'

'Exactly.'

'Gideon, stop saying exactly!'

'I'm impressed. You're beginning to think like me. Yes, this is a typical strategy. There's a list somewhere and Ivanovo is the 23rd word in it. All we have to do is find the list.' There was a hint of a smile as he added, 'Or rather, that's all *you* have to do.'

'Thank you.'

'It's gotta be in the encyclopedia somewhere.'

'Yeah, but I've got hundreds of lists in there - lists of rulers, sports winners... It could be any one of them. No, it's got to be more specific than that.'

It had started to rain. Holyhead Mountain had completely disappeared from view in the misty dark. No inspiration to be found there. Maybe if I prayed to the patron saint of cryptology, if there is one ... or encyclopedias ... St Isidore of Seville compiled an encyclopedia ... maybe he could help...

Gideon interrupted my reverie.

'You know... I've been thinking about what you said on the phone last night.'

'Which bit?'

'The bit about why our man sent out a second printing of the encyclopedia to his contacts, when there were hardly any changes in it.'

That was another thing that had been bugging me.

'Go on.'

'Well, maybe the reason lies in those changes. Maybe they're more significant than we thought. Let's take a look at Latvia.'

I reached over to the two printings of the encyclopedia, still lying on the table by my desk, and opened each at the Latvia page. It reminded me.

'Actually, Isidore...'

'Isidore?'

'Sorry, Gideon... I compared the two entries for Latvia last night, when I first started thinking about this. There's just one extra phrase added... here.' I pointed to the addition: 'independence talks with USSR, 1990'.

'There's an I word, for a start', said Gideon.

'And more to the point...' I typed furiously into my gematria program. 'Look. Yes! Independence scores 98.'

9

The next few pieces of the puzzle fell into place quite quickly. I looked up the word-lists scoring 98 in my gematria printout, and found those beginning with I:

> idealists, immaculate, impinging, improve, incunabula, independence, indication, indifference, infamous, inferences, infertile, inflexible, informer, inhabitant, innommable, inscribes, insulin, invested, invites, isomers, israelite, istanbul, ivanovo

Perfect. Ivanovo was 23. Then we found the scores for the other words in the phrase:

talks	63
with	60
USSR	77

We looked up the list for 63, found the words beginning with E, and counted down: the fourth one was 'eleven'. We did the same for S words in the 60 list: the 10th one was 'Sept'. And the 7th word in the T set at 77 was 'theater'. We wrote them out as a string, then rearranged them:

> Ivanovo theater, Sept 11

'That is what I call a neat bit of work', said Gideon.

Hilary came upstairs with some coffee. 'Why are you two grinning at each other?' she asked.

Gideon was ready with a reply. 'Oh, we just solved a marketing problem we were trying to get our heads around.'

'Can I see it?'

'Sure, in a bit. But it's not ready yet. We've still got some work to do on it.'

She turned to go back downstairs, and then stopped.

'Oh, I forgot.' She rummaged in her pocket. 'I found this envelope in our post box. It's for you. Must have been left there during the night. '

I took the envelope. It was addressed to David Crystal, c/o Uchelder Centre, in bold black type.

'That's odd. If someone wanted to send a message to me at Ucheldre, why didn't they leave it there instead of bringing it here?'

I shouted down to Hilary. 'When did it arrive?'

'Don't know exactly. Some time this afternoon.'

So the Centre would have been open. It didn't close until 5.

Gideon was looking at the envelope.

'What is this place? How on earth do you pronounce it?'

I sounded it out for him. Ich-**ell**-dre.

'Is that Welsh?'

'Yes. It means 'high town'. The Ucheldre Centre is a new community arts centre at the very top of the hill in Holyhead. Just round the corner. It's the highest point in the town.'

'So why this address? Are you involved in it?'

'Yes. I chair the management committee. We opened it just last year. It's an old convent chapel that the council was going to pull down, but a group of us got together to save it. We're planning to improve the facilities, build an extension, that sort of thing.'

I began opening the envelope.

'We've been asking local people for their support - and their ideas about how to develop it. So this is probably someone with a suggestion for an event. I've had a few messages like that already.'

But when I read the letter, it was different. Typed, for a start, even the signature.

> Dear Mr Crystal
> I was very pleased to hear about Ucheldre Centre, and I have ideas about fund-raising that I think will help a lot. Can we meet? I am not in Hollyhead very often, but I will be here next week, as I do something at Breakwater Park site. Perhaps we can meet there? You can leave a message for me at Trearddur Bay Hotel.

Yours faithfully
John Patterson

'Do you know this Patterson guy?' Gideon asked.

'Never heard of him. But it's great to hear of someone who can help with funding. That's our main problem at the moment. We're desperately short of cash.'

'That's very clever.'

'Huh?'

'I said that's very clever. Getting under your guard like that.'

'What? You mean you think this is a con? Something to do with the Soviets?'

'I told you. Anything unexpected, out of the ordinary. Watch out.'

'But this isn't really out of the ordinary. As I said, I do get messages quite often about Ucheldre.'

'But written like this?'

I had to admit I'd not seen one like that. Typed. Local people who were interested in the Centre just scribbled me a note. And they usually called me David. Or, if they were being very formal, Professor. Not usually Mr. And locals wouldn't spell Holyhead wrongly. They might mis-spell Ucheldre, but never Holyhead. He certainly wasn't a local man.

The stylistic part of my brain switched on. It was a curious style. Sounded a bit foreign. 'I do something'. A native speaker of English would have said 'I'm doing something'. And then there was the omission of 'the' before Ucheldre, Breakwater, and Trearddur. That's a typical error of Slavic speakers. There's no definite or indefinite article in ...

'... Russian.' Gideon finished off my last comment for me. 'I know Russian,' he added laconically. 'Part of the job.'

'So what should I do?'

'Well nothing, right now. There's something more important to do. We've got to decode Belorussia. We can decide what to do about Pattersonski afterwards.'

We began to repeat the procedure we carried out with Latvia, but this time using the 1991 reprint and comparing it to the proofs I'd just sent off to Cambridge. I'd not made any changes to the Byelorussian entry between the 1990 and 1991 printings. Nothing had happened then. But this last year had seen everything happening. This was the 1991 entry:

> **Belorussian SSR** (USSR) or **White Russia**, Russ **Belorussskaya** or **Belorussiya** SSR pop (1983) 9 807 000; area 207 600 sq km / 80 134 sq ml. Constituent republic of the Soviet Union, W European USSR, bounded W by Poland; largely flat, with low hills in the NW rising to 345 m/1 132 ft; chief rivers, the Dnieper, Zapadnaya Dvina, Neman; c.11 000 lakes; a third covered by forests; proclaimed a

Soviet Socialist Republic, 1919; capital, Minsk; chief towns, Gomel', Vitebsk, Mogilev, Bobruysk, Grodno, Brest; machine tools, vehicles, agricultural machinery, glass, foodstuffs, fertilizers, textiles, electronics, artificial silk, flax, and leather, oil extraction and refining, salt extraction; farmland covers 46% of the land area; meat and dairy production, flax. >> Minsk; Soviet Union

In the 1992 proof I'd had to make more than the usual changes, to avoid the page overrunning. An official name was now being reported (this was before the days when Belarus became widely used), so I had to include it along with its date: 'official name **Republic of Byelarus** (from 1991)'. This made the entry longer by a line, so something had to go, to keep the entry within its space. By taking out 'declaration of independence, 1990' and 'chief towns, Gomel', Vitebsk, Mogilev, Bobryusk, Grodno, Brest' everything fitted comfortably.

'This is a very different situation from Latvia', I said.

'Why so?'

'Latvia was a simple case of an additional few words. Here we've got words being deleted, and some part-substitutions. Look.'

I showed him the revised entry, and underlined the changes:

Belorussia or **White Russia**, Russ **Belorussskaya**, official name **Republic of Byelarus** (from 1991) Republic in NE Europe, bounded W by Poland; largely flat, with low hills in the NW rising to 345 m/1 132 ft; chief rivers, the Dnieper, Zapadnaya Dvina, Neman; c.11 000 lakes; a third covered by forests; proclaimed a Soviet Socialist Republic, 1919; declaration of independence, 1990; capital, Minsk; chief towns, Gomel', Vitebsk, Mogilev, Bobruysk, Grodno, Brest; machine tools, vehicles, agricultural machinery, glass, foodstuffs, fertilizers, textiles, electronics, artificial silk, flax, and leather, oil extraction and refining, salt extraction; farmland covers 46% of the land area; meat and dairy production, flax. >> Minsk; Soviet Union

'See. That first sentence. 'Constituent republic of the Soviet Union, W European USSR' has gone, and instead we've got 'Republic in NE Europe'. What do we do with that?'

Gideon thought for a moment. 'If I was constructing this code, I wouldn't want to make it too complicated. Our guy's contacts will want something straightforward. We know who they are. None of them have a background in cryptology. And the code is pretty well hidden already.'

'So what are you saying?'

'The simplest thing would be to let all changes count - anything, addition or deletion. As long as there's a new word added, or an old word left out, it's able to be coded.'

'So that means we don't count 'republic', as it turns up in both entries?'

'Right. And in fact, now I'm, thinking along these lines, there are some other things we should discount.'

'Like what?'

Well, those little words, like 'of'. They're likely too short to produce results.'

'Grammatical words.'

'What?'

'Linguists call them grammatical words. They show the structure of a sentence.'

Gideon's face told me that I wasn't helping.

'But we allowed in 'with' when we were doing Latvia', I added.

'Yeah, but there were only four words in that phrase, and our man needed them all. In a longer example, like we've got here, words like 'with' would get in the way.'

'So we leave them out, for the time being.'

'Yeah. Numbers too. Like 1990. This code is based on letters, not numbers, I'm sure of that.'

'So I ignore 1983 becoming 1989.'

'Exactly. And I'm also pretty sure that titles of entries don't count either.'

'What do you mean, titles?'

'The stuff at the beginning of the entry. The words in bold face and their glosses. Some of them aren't English words, for a start, and abbreviations like *Russ* are ambiguous. The contacts wouldn't know whether to read it as *Russ* or *Russian*?'

'Same with abbreviations then, I suppose.'

'Yeah. Look, *NE* turns up in one entry and not in the other. Would that be coded N + E or as North + East? Too ambiguous. Ignore it.'

'OK. Ignore.'

'Ignore for now, I mean. I might be wrong, in any of this. But I don't think I am. No, concentrate just on the text in the entries.'

'Right. Drink your coffee while I sort this out.'

I copied the proof entry into Word and deleted all the text apart from the changes between the two versions. I ended up with a list of 16 items. I showed them to Gideon.

> constituent, Soviet, Union, European, USSR, declaration, independence, chief, towns, Gomel, Vitebsk, Mogilev, Bobryusk, Grodno, Brest

'It's rather a lot', I said.

'Well, maybe the message has to be longer this time, for some reason. Doesn't matter. The important thing is to decode it. Get your gematria thingy onto it. I'll divide the Belorussia character string into groups.'

That didn't take long. I've still got the table I wrote out, putting in the gematria totals and Gideon's groups. We ordered them exactly as they appeared in the string, just as we'd done for Latvia. The paper's full of creases, because of the way I'd scrunged it up, but I found it later in the wastepaper basket and decided to keep it as a sort of memento of the way things can go wrong. I see I used G for gematria.

Word	*G value*	*Place in G list*	*Result*
Gomel	52	A05	
chief	31	A05	
constituent	160	S08	
Mogilev	83	S30	
declaration	102	C24	
Vitebsk	88	G02	
towns	91	E19	
Bobryusk	113	C31	
USSR	77	B23	
Brest	64	B04	
Grodno	73	L37	
independence	98	T07	
Europe	80	H17	
Soviet	90	E04	
European	95	F07	

I got out my lists of gematria equivalent words and began to fill in the table. I hadn't felt so - excited? nervous? I couldn't tell - in ages. Gideon was tapping the table, finger at a time, as if it was a piano.

The 5th word beginning with A for value 52...

Gomel	52	A05	adverb

We both spoke at the same time. 'Adverb?' Gideon looked at me with a quizzical expression, but I was as taken aback as he was.

'Well, maybe when there's a lot of words to take into account, not all the words are needed, so he puts in some irrelevant words... like parts of speech ...' My voice tailed off. It seemed a pretty thin reason.

The 5th word beginning with A for value 31...

Gomel	52	A05	adverb
chief	31	A05	-

There was no such word. Only two words began with A in the list.

I tried the same reasoning again. Perhaps that was OK. Maybe with a long message not all words would be given a gloss. The explanation seemed even thinner.

Next was the 8th word beginning with S for value 160...

Gomel	52	A05	adverb
chief	31	A05	-

constituent	160	S08	Stringfellow

We looked at each other.

'He's a nightclub owner. Well, a gentlemen's club, as they say.'

Gideon pursed his lips. 'That doesn't seem a very likely meeting place.'

I agreed. 'The Soviet Union and lap dancing don't seem a natural fit.'

We added the rest of the words in an increasingly gloomy silence. At the end the table looked like this:

Gomel	52	A05	adverb
chief	31	A05	-
constituent	160	S08	Stringfellow
Mogilev	83	S30	squalid
declaration	102	C24	concertina
Vitebsk	88	G02	gamester
towns	91	E19	excerpt
Bobryusk	113	C31	-
USSR	77	B23	briefly
Brest	64	B04	balletic
Grodno	73	L14	Llanfair
independence	98	T07	tendencies
Europe	80	H17	-
Soviet	90	E04	elkhound
European	95	F07	fictions

Despite the gloom, Gideon burst out laughing at 'concertina'. 'They're even planning to have music now'. And I managed a wry smile at 'Llanfair'.

'It's a village just down the road from here. Famous.'

'Why?'

'It's the longest place-name in the country. Llanfair is just the first part of it. It means 'Mary's church'. The whole thing is 58 letters. Took up nearly two lines in the encyclopedia.'

'Can you say it?'

'Of course. It's a rite of passage round here.'

So I said it. Well, it was something to say. Neither of us wanted to voice what was in our minds. Then Gideon did.

'It's not working.'

'No.'

I tried to make a joke. 'A pity. I love the thought of a group of spies meeting in Llanfairpwllgwyngyllgogerychwyrndrobwllllanty siliogogogoch.' Gideon tried to smile, and failed.

It couldn't possibly be right. Apart from the random look of the words, there were three places where we'd had blanks. There weren't 5 words beginning with C at value 31 or 31 words beginning with C at value 113 or 17 words beginning with H at value 80. And yet the method seemed to work for Latvia. It didn't make sense. I screwed up the list and threw it into the wastepaper basket.

We were, it seemed, back to square one. It was getting late. We had run out of mental energy, and Patterson's letter still had to be dealt with. We agreed to think about that the next day.

We'd meet in the morning. Gideon went back to his b&b. It would be another fitful night's sleep for both of us.

10

'You have to meet him', said Gideon.

It was 11 o'clock on Saturday, the 4th. The office was empty apart from the two of us. Hilary was out doing some weekend shopping. The kids were - I don't know - out somewhere ...

'It's not going to go away, you know. You can't bury your head in the sand and pretend it isn't happening.'

'That's exactly what I want to do.' I'd been imagining all sorts of scenarios, most of them influenced by Le Carré, all of them with an unhappy ending.

'Is there any way out of it?'

'Only one. If you crack that code, and we let them know we're onto them, then they'll leave you alone. They'll be too busy trying to reorganise themselves.'

'I can't see any way to break that code. We gave it our best shot.'

'Give it another best shot.'

I reached down into the wastepaper basket, and took out the scrunged list, smoothed it out, then crushed it again.

'I'll have a go, but I'm not optimistic. It'll take time.'

'Then we play for time. Give Patterson a call, and say you're away or something until the middle of next week. Or too busy. That'll give me time too.'

'For what?'

'Oh...' Gideon looked evasively at the window. 'Just to let me put some er... contingency measures in place.'

'Contingency measures.'

'Of course.'

I didn't press him, but my Le Carré thoughts had taken off. Tinker, Tailor, Editor, Spy... There's a rotten apple, Jim... Maybe I should take off my glasses and clean them with my tie. That's what George Smiley would do in my situation. I had an idea for a book. Dramatic Pause in Conversation, something like that.

If I lived long enough to write it...

I threw the paper ball back into the bin.

'OK. I'll give the hotel a call.'

'Do it now.'

'He won't be there.'

'That's fine. Just leave a message. Say you'll meet him at this Park place on ... don't leave it too long ... Tuesday?'

I nodded.

'Midday ... in the museum building'

I called the hotel. Yes, they knew about Mr Patterson, and yes, they were expecting him on Sunday, and yes, I could leave a message. And a Happy New Year.

A new sense of the word 'happy', I thought.

'Right,' said Gideon. 'I'll leave you to it.' He got up to go downstairs, then turned. 'Remember what I said about these guys. They're not cryptologists. They wouldn't be able to handle anything too difficult. Whatever we're missing, it'll be something really obvious.'

I sat down at my computer and called up the Belorussia entry. Maybe I'd missed out some words? I went through the entry again, minutely ... no ... I'd noted all the changes. I looked at the words Gideon had told me to omit, like the grammatical words. It took me the rest of the morning to calculate the values of all of them, and look them up in my gematria lists, but none of them threw any further light on the situation. The gematria equivalents were just as meaningless.

Hilary had come back from her shopping trip. 'Gideon gone?'

'Yeah.'

'Is he coming back?'

'No, not today.' I realized I wasn't sure when I would see him again. All he'd said, when he left, was 'Call me'.

'So is the marketing issue all sorted?'

'Not entirely. I've still got some work to do on the er...' - what had I told her? - quizzes.' That's the problem with lies. You have to remember what you've said before. It's how suspects get caught out. They change their story.

'Can I see them? I'm good at quizzes.'

'Oh sure, when I've got a draft in reasonable shape.'

'Have you got a deadline?'

'Er ... yes. Next ... Tuesday.'

'Oh good. So you'll have time for a walk?'

Hilary loved to go on walks. Still does. And I've usually got so much on that I stay at home. But actually, this time, a bit of fresh air, I thought, would probably do me good. Might even give me some ideas.

'Sure. Where shall we go?'

'Oh anywhere. Why not the Breakwater Park?'

'The Breakwater Park!'

'Don't sound so surprised. Be interesting to see what they're up to, now it's been opened for a while.'

It wasn't surprise, I wanted to tell her. I settled for a bland 'Good idea.'

It takes about half an hour to walk from our house to the Park. There's a path that takes you over the lower part of Holyhead Mountain and down towards the sea. It's called Rocky Coast by the locals. Very important to keep turning right. If you turn left, you start going up the mountain, and if you're not careful you end up at the top of the quarry cliffs.

That's what makes the Breakwater Park so special. The backdrop of the sheer cliff walls, 300 feet high. The quarry was formed in the mid-1800s, when stone was needed to build the long breakwater, to protect Holyhead harbour. It ended up over a mile and a half in length - 'the longest breakwater in Europe', people say, and after a few drinks, 'in the world' - and took millions of tons of stone. I remember, when I was a kid, growing up in Holyhead, a quarry engine trundling along the breakwater carrying rocks to repair the damage caused by the ferocious gales. In Victorian times it attracted visitors from all over the country, including the royal family. A spectacular walk, whatever the weather.

That day in January it had rained a bit in the morning, but it had cleared by lunchtime. It was cold, though. As we put on our coats, Queen echoed down the stairs. ... I'm just a poor boy, I need no sympathy ... Better put on boots too. It can be very muddy along the coast. But boots are never where you want them to be. By the time I'd found mine, the Rhapsody was almost over ... Just gotta get right outta here ...

We got out just before Queen started to sing again. As we walked along the long road leading to the park, the tall chimney of the old brick works came into view. A good place to meet Patterson? There was a new museum nearby, so there would be people around. I didn't want to find myself in an isolated place with him - though I didn't suppose Gideon would let that happen.

On the way back we met him walking towards the Park. He was being a tourist, he told Hilary, with a sunny smile. Yeah, right, I thought.

I don't think I noticed the scenery much that day. My mind was flitting between codes and moles ... Richman, Poorman, Editor, Thief. ... It had become an earworm. But I do remember paying particular attention to the layout of the buildings in the Park. There was the old brick shed and the building where the raw materials to make the bricks were crushed. The small museum opposite. Good to see that the notices were in both English and Welsh. A small lake, well populated with ducks and - being the weekend - a couple of model-boat enthusiasts. A stone path led up towards the North Stack at the end of Holyhead Mountain.

We walked the other way, along Rocky Coast, and then up through the town and back to the house. There was an envelope lying on the mat inside the front door. I froze. Hilary picked it up and opened it.

'It's an invitation.'

'From who?' I said guardedly.

'Holyhead Opportunities Trust.'

'Ah.' That was OK. HOT had been formed a couple of years before to help regenerate the town. Holyhead had come bottom of an economic league table in 1988, labelled 'the most depressed town in Britain'. HOT was formed to do something about it. I was one of the twelve trustees. We met regularly to discuss new projects - the Ucheldre Centre was one - and evidently the HOT organizers felt that a social evening would be good for morale.

'When is it?'

'Next Saturday. Are you free?'

'I hope - ' I corrected myself quickly. 'I expect so. Are you?'

'I'm not invited.'

I looked at the invitation. 'Yes you are. Well, sort of. Look at the wording.'

Someone had written on the invitation: DAVID CRYSTAL PLUS ONE.

Hilary looked puzzled. 'What does *plus one* mean?'

It was a fairly new usage, becoming very fashionable in the 1980s, but it was the first time we'd met it personally. We weren't party-going animals.

'It means the person invited is allowed to bring one other person with them.'

'Like a wife.'

'Or a mistress... anybody...'

I ducked as a boot came in my direction.

'Darling ... you are definitely my plus-one.'

Then I froze. Hilary looked at me.

'What's the matter?'

'It's plus-one!'

'I know.'

'Sorry ... just thought of something ... must go and check it in that quiz I've been working on.'

As I ran upstairs, two at a time, the phrase pounded in my head. It seemed to get louder and louder. Plus one. Plus One. PLUS ONE.'

11

Gideon had said it would be something obvious, and so it was. We'd overlooked the simplest thing. The message in the latest letter didn't say *Belorussia*. It said *Belorussia +1.* I suppose I'd thought the plus sign meant 'one extra person', or 'one additional country', or something like that. And Gideon hadn't remarked on it either. But it was much more basic. Every instinct now told me it was a gematria clue.

I got out my old list, and added 1 to each of the numbers, and checked them off, one by one, in the wordlists.

The 5th word under A for value 53...

Gomel	53	A05	affirm

The 5th word under A for value 32...

Gomel	53	A05	affirm
chief	32	A05	agenda

In no time, it seemed, the table was complete.

Gomel	53	A05	affirm
chief	32	A05	agenda
constituent	161	S07	supranational
Mogilev	84	S30	states

declaration	103	C24	committee
Vitebsk	89	G02	gathering
towns	92	E19	established
Bobryusk	114	C31	Cottesloe
USSR	78	B23	building
Brest	65	B04	Bankside
Grodno	74	L14	London
independence	99	T07	thirteen
Europe	81	H17	hours
Soviet	91	E04	eleventh
European	96	F07	February

I phoned Gideon immediately - but there was no reply. Still wandering around the Breakwater Park, I assumed. I left a message on his phone. 'I've cracked it.' Then, still not quite believing what I was seeing, I went back to my lists and checked through all the values again. Confirmed.

I put the table into a drawer and began to go downstairs, then stopped. Hilary would be wanting an explanation for my excitement. I spent a couple of minutes cooking up another quiz question - not a brilliant one, but I thought it would work.

She was in the sitting room. 'What was that about?"

'Oh yes. Perfect. It was the one answer I was looking for.'

'I still don't know what you're talking about.'

'My last quiz question. The anagram phrase I needed .'

'Anagram?'

'I've got seven letters ELNOPSU and I need an anagram that makes sense for the clue I've got. And *one plus* works. I was getting alternatives that didn't make much sense, like *pen soul*.'

'And *no pulse*.'

'Hadn't thought of that one. But *one plus* is really good, so I've used it.'

It wasn't a brilliant explanation, but it would have to do. It was getting late, and there were two young and hungry mouths to feed. We ordered a takeaway.

We'd not long finished when Gideon called.

'You really did it?

'Yep. Let me tell you.'

He cut in. 'Not on the phone. I'll be right round.'

And he was. Nearer five than ten minutes this time. We went into the study and I closed the door.

I got the table out. 'There.'

Gideon read it carefully.

'You're sure? No errors?'

I shook my head.

'Well, then. Congratulations. How did you do it?'

'I read something that made me realise what that plus sign meant. Flash of inspiration. Is it the sort of thing you were hoping for?

'Oh yes.' Gideon sounded quite emotional.

'It's quite a long message, though. Very wordy.'

'Yeah, but that's a consequence of the method. Once our man had chosen Belorussia, he was committed to using all the changed words in the entry. It must have taken him quite a while to find the right entry.'

'Oh, I don't know. There are so many alternatives for any one gematria value that I reckon it wouldn't take more than an hour or so to cook up a plausible message. As you said, it has to be simple. It's the sort of thing I do for the after-dinner speeches I was telling you about. It doesn't take long to find a convincing message. We could do it now if you like.'

Gideon was fascinated. 'Go on, then.'

'Well, you choose the message.'

'Say I want to meet you somewhere near here.'

'OK. Let's go to Armenia.'

I put the two books side by side. 'You time me.'

'Right. It's 8.30 now.'

It took me five minutes to find the differences. Just three bits changed. I underlined the ten significant words.

declaration of independence as the republic of Armenia
including the holy mountain of Ararat
independence talks with USSR, 1990

Putting them through the gematria software took about a minute. I wrote them out as we'd done before.

declaration	102
independence	98
republic	86
Armenia	61
including	93
holy	60
mountain	107
Ararat	59
talks	63
USSR	77

'Now... this is the slowest bit.' I went to 98 first, as I'd done that before, for Belorussia, and I remembered noticing ...

'There we are. 98 Crystal.'

Gideon spluttered. 'You're kidding.'

'Not in the least. Check it out yourself. Here's a list of letter values.'

He took the list and went down it. C = 3. Plus R = 18. Plus Y = 25 ... He got to L, and looked at me with what seemed to be fresh respect.

'98', he said apologetically.

I began to go through the other values. The trick is to find one crucial word and then relate the others to it. In 77 I found valley. Valley is the name of a village just a couple of miles from Holyhead. Then in 60 I found hotel. There is a Valley Hotel. An excellent meeting place. The rest was easy, as there were lots of possible choices using general words such as 'approve' and 'next'. In the end I gave him this list:

USSR	77	valley
holy	60	hotel
including	93	approve
Armenia	61	official
declaration	102	scheduling
independence	98	crystal
republic	86	nineteen
mountain	107	twenty
Ararat	59	third
talks	63	next

'There you are, Gideon. We meet at 7 in the evening on the 23rd January at the Valley Hotel.'

Gideon looked at his watch. 'and that took just over an hour. Impressive.'

'A bit less, probably, as we spent a few minutes being sidetracked over Crystal.'

Gideon raised both hands in the air in a gesture of submission. 'Ya podchinyayus.'

'What?'

'I surrender.'

He looked again at the Belorussia list.

'What is this Cottesloe place?'

'It's one of the theatres inside the National Theatre. An odd place to have a meeting.'

'Not if you're part of a Global Shakespeare Association. It's the perfect cover. Nobody would think twice about it.'

'But this is the UK, not Russia. Will they all be able to get here?'

'Oh yes. They'll probably use their diplomatic status to get themselves ino the country.'

He got up. 'And now I've got some work to do.'

'What's the next step?'

'First thing is to check out the Cottesloe for the 11th February. Our man in Cambridge must have arranged it already. What day of the week is that?'

I looked at the calendar on the study wall. 'A Tuesday.'

'And it's afternoon. 1 o'clock. So there won't be a show on.'

'I shouldn't think so. Not at that time. Hang on. I can tell you. I get the NT stuff sent to me.'

I rummaged around in another drawer and found the flyer. 'Angels in America' starts later this month. Evening performance on the 11th.'

'So the theatre should be empty - if they're using the theatre, that is. More likely he's booked one of the rooms nearby.'

We went downstairs. At the front door, Gideon shook my hand. 'Thanks for all that. Great piece of work.'

'When will I next see you?' Patterson was on my mind again.

'Not tomorrow. I've got too much arranging to do. Monday. I'll call you.'

I watched him walk to the gate. As he reached it, he turned. 'And don't worry.'

I waved, but it wasn't a wave of agreement. It was going to be a long time till Tuesday.

12

I spent most of Sunday thinking about what Gideon would do next - which really meant what *I* would do if I were him. As far as I could see, he had two options. He could let the meeting go ahead, and bug it in some way so that we could find out what the group was up to. I realized I was thinking 'we'. I meant 'they'. Gideon and his department, whatever it was. He'd never told me. ...

Or he could stop the meeting taking place. All he'd have to do is let the various contacts know they were onto them, and that the Cambridge mole's cover was blown. But then they might just reconvene in some other way, without the mole. Unlikely. If Gideon was right about the UN schedule, they would need to make a quick decision. There just wouldn't be time. ...

I was convinced by his assassination scenario. You didn't need a degree in politics to work out that there'd be a lot of people who were hotly opposed to the break-up of the Soviet Union, and who wanted to do something about it. And some of them would be very powerful figures in their countries. The old Soviet network would still be alive, operating out of the public eye as it always did. So they'd got together to plan - what, some sort of coup? And assassination could well be a part of that...

Gideon wouldn't be able to make that kind of decision alone. It would have to be a top-level security judgement. Control and the Minister, sort of thing, as Le Carré would say. Would he be able to reach all the relevant people on a Sunday? Intelligence never sleeps, according to the spy novels, and I didn't suppose most of the key players were church-goers ...

The Lord be with you. And with your spirit. I realized I hadn't heard a word of the two Epistles I was supposed to have been listening to. And here was the Gospel already, the story about the three wise men visiting Jesus and bringing him presents. From the East. It was the Feast of the Epiphany, transferred from the following day. Twelfth Night.

As I stood up, I glanced around the Church. The 11 o'clock Mass at Saint Mary's was fuller than usual. A few visitors still on holiday, all of them with families I knew. At the very back, someone I didn't recognize. For a moment I thought it was Gideon, but it wasn't, though there was something about the way he was sitting that reminded me of him. He was so clearly not looking in my direction that it seemed deliberate. Or was this my imagination? A Moscow Centre-trained hood if ever I saw one, Mr Smiley. Or was it Mr Guillam? Never mind. Where were we? Ah yes, men from the East. And King Herod trying to get information out of them about where the child was. 'And having been warned in a dream not to return to Herod, they left for their own country by another road.' I could do with a dream like that, I thought. Something that would tell me what to do.

Two options. No, there was a third. They could simply disappear the mole and replace him with a British agent who could continue sending messages of some sort. I'd learned that use of the verb during the 1970s, when it began to be used about opponents of political regimes in South America who had simply vanished ... transitive use of 'disappear' ... unusual ... common enough now, though ... Three options, then ... was there a fourth? I went through the first two options again. Surely they'd want to listen in to the meeting. That's what Gideon had said they wanted to do, after all. But then what? After they'd learned whatever the plot was, what would they do? Arrest them? No, they were diplomats of a sort. And would the British government want a diplomatic incident? Or maybe - Let us offer each other a sign of peace.

It was the point in the Mass where people turned to each other and shook hands, and wished each other 'peace' - or 'tangnefedd' in Welsh. Some would exchange a kiss. As I turned to greet the person sitting behind me, I looked again at the back row. The stranger wasn't there. Disappeared.

When Mass was over, I button-holed Jimmy, the man who took the collection. He always sat at the back.

'Who was that guy sitting along the row from you, Jimmy?'

'I dunno. Never saw him before.'

'When did he leave?'

'Not sure. When I went up with the collection he was there. When I got back he wasn't. Probably not feeling well.'

I turned to leave, when Jimmy added.

'Funny chap, though. He didn't join in at all. Didn't stand up when we all did, and so on. It was as if he'd not been to Mass before.'

No, I thought. I don't suppose he had.

When we got home, I called Gideon.

'This may be a coincidence, but...' and told him what had happened.

'Can you describe him?'

I did my best. I'm not good at describing people. Not like Charles Dickens, who could paint a picture of a person in words so brilliantly. 'Looked a bit like you', was the best I could come up with.'

But it seems that was enough. 'Ah, that'll be Errol.'

'Errol?'

'Yes, he's one of ours. I called him last night, and he drove up straight away. I told him to keep an eye on you.'

'How did he know I'd be at Mass?'

'David...' I detected a tone of disappointment. 'We're not amateurs. We've done our homework, you know.'

Of course they had. They probably knew more about me than I knew myself.

'Just ignore him, if you see him again. He'll ignore you. You might see him near your house.'

'He'll stand out a bit, won't he? It's a very quiet street.'

'Oh, don't worry about that. They're very good at blending into the background.'

'They?'

'Yes. Didn't I say? There's a small team coming up to help keep an eye on things. They'll be in place by the end of today.'

'Oh.'

'I told you. I'm going to keep you safe. Enjoy the rest of your Sunday.'

I tried. A trip to the cinema was being mooted by the family. Good idea. Something nice and funny would take my mind off things, away from encyclopedias, and codes, and alphabets. What was on? 'There's a new release which looks fun,' said Lucy. Splendid. What is it? An Agatha Christie story. Poirot. 'The ABC Murders'.

No escape.

I enjoyed the film, I have to say, and it stayed with me. That night I dreamed of spies being killed, but instead of ABC railway guides being left beside each victim, there was a copy of the Cambridge Encyclopedia, and because my picture was on it the police thought I did it. One of the tabloids had a big picture of me and the headline 'Tinker, Tailor, Editor, Spy-killer'. I was in court about to be sentenced when I woke up.

Something had woken me up. The sound of hammering. I looked out of the bedroom window. It was right by our house, on our side of the road. A small van, a Punch-and-Judy-shaped tent, and a prominent 'men at work' road sign. Took up half the road. The staff would have problems parking when they arrived for work.

Something up with the telephones, it seemed. The van had one of the new British Telecom logos on it - a leaping red and blue piper next to a big BT. There's a telegraph pole on the corner, with lines going to several houses. We'd had quite a strong wind a few days before. Maybe one of the lines had come down. It wasn't ours, though. I picked up our phone to see if it was working. Our office uses phones a lot. There was a normal dialling tone. Still, worth a check, to see if we were going to have problems later in the day. I'd go out and ask the men as soon as I was dressed.

Change of plan. A workman came out of the tent. It was the man I'd seen at the back of the church. What did Gideon call him? Eryl? Errol? So that was it. Gideon's team had arrived. He spoke to whoever was doing the hammering and went to sit in the front of the van. I was fascinated. So this is what surveillance was like. After a few minutes the noise stopped and the hammerer appeared from where he'd been working. A complete contrast with Eryl/Errol. Smaller build, wiry ... perfect for climbing up telegraph poles, or for ...

'Are you coming down for breakfast? Hilary came into the bedroom. 'What's so interesting?'

'Just wondering what those guys are up to.'

She went to open up the office. It was going to be a routine day, as far as the encyclopedia team were concerned. We had a meeting at 11, to discuss how we were going to plan the new books. It would take quite a lot of thought, as we'd need separate storage areas on our computers and a huge amount of coordination. The worst thing, with team editing, is if someone changes an entry and the others don't know about it. Then if someone else changes the original entry, we have two new versions that aren't in sync. We'd got a system in place to prevent that happening with the big encyclopedia. Now we had to repeat the process for the Concise edition.

It was reassuring having Errol/Eryl and 'Stan' outside - I'd decided that was his name, as the two men had a vague resemblance to Laurel and Hardy - and I found I was able to concentrate more than I was expecting. Until the phone rang.

'Hello?'

The voice at the other end sounded slightly foreign.

'Is that Mr Crystal?'

'Yes.'

'I am so sorry to trouble you. This is Mr Patterson. I got your message.'

'Ah. Good morning.'

Gideon... where are you when I need you?

'Yes. Good morning.'

There was a pause, as if he was waiting for me to say something.

'I am really sorry but my plans have to change and I must leave here tomorrow. Can we meet today perhaps?'

Play for time ... play for time ... need time to call Gideon ...

'Well I think that might be possible. I've got a meeting in the office this morning, but I should think that early this afternoon might be all right ...'

'That would be perfect. We shall meet in the same place? At Breakwater Park?'

'In the museum, yes. Shall we say three o'clock?'

'I shall see you in museum at that time. Thank you, Mr Crystal.'

'Thank you, Mr Patterson. It's good of you to be thinking of our Ucheldre Centre.'

There was a pause.

'Yes. I do not know if I can be of much help, but I have some ideas.'

'Thank you again.'

We exchanged polite goodbyes, then I went downstairs, out of earshot of the office, to use a different phone. I knew Gideon's number by heart. He answered straight away.

'I've just tried to call you, but you were engaged.'

'It was Patterson.'

'Patterson?'

'Yes. He says he has to leave tomorrow and wants to meet me later today at the Park.'

'When?'

'Three.'

I could hear Gideon thinking.

'Right. I'm not entirely surprised.'

'What do you mean?'

'It's a standard ruse. Get an appointment set up and then change it at the last minute. If the mark has suspected something, and set up some protection, it's not going to be of any use.'

'Oh.'

'But what Patterson doesn't know is that we're already onto him. I'll just bring our arrangements forward.'

'So I keep the appointment.'

'Most certainly. But don't agree if you hear from him again wanting a further change.'

'OK.'

'And when you meet him, keep close to the museum. He'll want to take you somewhere out of the public eye. No going for walks up the mountain or anything like that.'

'OK.'

'And if you see any of us, ignore us. We'll be watching you, but we don't want you watching us.'

'OK.'

'See you there. And don't worry.'

'I won't,' I said, in a tone that I hoped sounded convincing. 'By the way, what were you calling me about?'

'Oh just to let you know that we've been doing some checking with the Nationl Theatre. Somebody from Cambridge has booked a room by the Cottesloe for a special meeting of the Global Shakespeare Association. February 11th. As predicted.'

'Great.'

'Thought you'd be pleased.'

And I suppose I was, in a half-hearted sort of way.

13

I didn't eat much lunch, and my nervouness showed. Hilary asked me if I was feeling all right. I explained it away as work-related preoccupation, after our morning meeting. Also, I said, I was wondering about my afternoon meeting. After Patterson's phone call, I'd told her about his Ucheldre idea. She was as intrigued as I had been - but for different reasons.

I left in my car at 2.30. It was only a five-minute drive, but I wanted to be there in good time. As I pulled out of the drive, I looked up the road. The workmen's tent was still there, and the fenced off area, but not their van. And no sign of any telephone activity.

I bumped into the Breakwater Park warden as I parked outside the museum building. I knew him, as we'd met a few times when working with Holyhead Opportunities Trust on the regeneration of the area. 'What are you doing here, David?' he asked.

'Oh, just meeting someone,' I replied as nonchalantly as I could.

'Mr Patterson?'

I had read the expression 'I nearly jumped out of my skin' often enough in novels, but this was the first time I got an inkling of what it might feel like.

'Ye - yes. How do you know him?'

'Well he's meeting me this afternoon too. After you. I expect you got a call like I did.'

Gosh, this guy's cover is good, I thought.

'Yeah. Do you know anything about him?'

'No. Sounds like some sort of entrepreneur. He seems to know about partnerships and funding and that sort of thing.'

'Well we both need that, certainly.'

We chatted a bit about grants and bureaucracy, then I looked at my watch. It was 2.50. 'Well, must get in. He's not arrived?'

'Not as far as I know. We are quite busy today, unusually. But if he's there he hasn't introduced himself. You can use my office, if you like.'

I went in to the museum. There were half a dozen people in the room, looking at the various posters and maps on the walls. Two of them I recognized: Eryl/Errol and 'Stan'. The other four seemed to be genuine tourists - two men who looked like climbers, and two ladies with a dog. No sign of Gideon.

The room housing the museum was quite small. A rectangular building, with stone walls and a slate roof. Inside, just one floor, with a small office at the end. A seawater fish tank. It's the same today, except that there is much more information about the local wildlife, and the Internet has made its presence felt. I went and stood by the office door. And waited.

The two ladies with their dog left after a few minutes, and almost immediately the door opened. I took a deep breath. But it was another climber, looking for his friends. They began to discuss routes to the best climbing locations. Gideon's associates ignored them, their attention totally taken up, it appeared, by a poster informing them about Anglesey geology. I was very impressed by their appearance. Cameras and notebooks. Not at all like the two workmen fixing our telegraph pole. They probably had various changes of clothing in their van.

By ten past three I was beginning to wonder if Patterson was going to show. Eryl/Errol and 'Stan' had finished looking at all the posters and were starting again. Then through the window I saw a black Mercedes tentatively looking for the car park. Very appropriate car, I thought.

Patterson came in looking flustered, and peered at everybody in the room before spotting me. He came over in a rush, and was full of apologies. I was Mr Crystal? He was John Patterson. He was so sorry to keep me waiting. A previous meeting had overrun, and he wasn't sure of the way to Breakwater Park ...

While he chattered on, I found it difficult to believe what I was seeing. A small man, almost hidden in a dufflecoat that seemed a couple of sizes too large for him ... thin-rimmed glasses ... a neatly trimmed moustache ... carrying a briefcase ... I took in these details before noticing the most relevant feature of all. He must have been 70, maybe more. A Moscow-trained hood? I know George Smiley was getting on for 60, but this was ridiculous.

The surprise must have shown on my face.

'Is there something wrong?' asked Patterson.

'N- nothing. Nothing at all. Erm... would you like to talk in here?' I gestured to the warden's office.

'No, here it is too noisy.' The climbers were debating the best way to climb to the top of the quarry cliffs, and in the small room their voices were quite a distraction.

'We could perhaps go outside to where the old buildings are?'

Well at least this part was what Gideon had predicted. We walked towards the door. I happened to catch Errol/Eryl's eye. He looked as puzzled as I did.

It was a mild day, for early January, and the sun actually made a brief appearance as we walked across the car park. The old buildings, as Patterson had called them, were being turned into an exhibition area, with wall panels describing the history of the quarry, and some surviving pieces of quarry eqipment. A lonely wagon stood on a segment of railway track. We sat down on a bench. Eryl/Errol and 'Stan' sauntered across to look at the panels while we did so. Very clearly in earshot.

As we talked, it dawned on me. Patterson was - genuine. He had visited Holyhead as a child. His mother had grown up here, and went to school in the Convent run by an order of French nuns. She became a teacher, and met her husband while working in the newly independent Czechoslovakia just after the end of the First World War. That's where Patterson was brought up, and he'd lived there ever since, apart from his travels abroad as a businessman.

All of this came out in response to my first question - why he was interested in the Ucheldre Centre. And as he told his story it all made perfect sense. The Centre was the old Convent chapel, refurbished as an arts centre, the only part of the old Convent still standing. Czech was Patterson's first language - he even apologized for his English at one point - which explained the linguistic things I'd noticed in his letter. Czech is a close relative of Russian.

He wanted to do something for Holyhead, as a memorial to his mother, who had recently died, so he had been visiting some of the tourist sites. He didn't have money himself, but he was connected with people who had - philanthropists interested in the arts. He gave me a list of names and said I should write to them, and mention his name. In my confused state, I think I said I most certainly would, and thanked him profusely. The whole conversation took less than a quarter of an hour, and then he was off, into the museum, for his meeting with the warden.

I looked around for Eryl/Errol and 'Stan'. They'd disappeared. Back to their telecom workmen role, I supposed. I began to wonder if this whole thing was a charade. All that nervousness for nothing. When I got home, I'd give Gideon a call and ask him what he thought was going on.

But when I did arrive back, all charade-like thoughts were crushed by what had happened in my absence.

14

Hilary looked up as I entered the office.

'Glad you're back. It's been all go while you've been out.'

'What's up?'

'Someone from BBC TV. They're planning a tourist programme on Anglesey, and they'll be up at South Stack tomorrow. They want someone to talk about the Hut Circles, and they thought of you.'

'Why me?'

'Well, you did it once before, and they've seen the footage.'

That was true. I'd been interviewed there a couple of years earlier for a programme about endangered languages. The producer wanted somewhere atmospheric to talk about the crisis affecting the world's languages. Half of them are so seriously endangered that they're likely to die out over the next hundred years. Was Welsh safe? That's what they wanted me to talk about. The remains of a third-century Celtic village were an ideal setting. And I did know quite a lot about them - it was actually my favourite part of Holy Island, and I'd always bring visitors to see them whenever I got the chance.

'And,' Hilary went on, 'You've had a delivery.'

There was a parcel on my desk.

'What is it?'

'I don't know. It's addressed to you, and it says Personal.'

'Well I've not ordered anything.'

'Nor have I. It must be a book from someone.'

'There's nothing to say who it's from.'

That was odd. Usually, when a book arrived from a colleague or a publisher, there would be a sender's name and address somewhere on the package. But this one had nothing, apart from a few spidery marks on the back.

I put it on one side. 'I'll open it in a minute,' I said, and changed the subject. 'Had a great meeting.' I told her about Patterson and his ideas, and showed her the list of names he'd given me. All very promising, she thought. We'd write some letters that evening.

'So what about the TV people?'

'Oh sure.' I didn't want to miss any chance to talk about the Welsh language situation, and this felt like another opportunity. 'What time would it be?'

'They didn't say. I said I'd call them back. I wasn't sure whether you wanted to do it.'

'Yes. I'll do it. I expect it'll have to be in the morning. The light's awful in the afternoon, especially if it's grey like today. Not first thing, though.'

As Hilary made her call, I looked at the parcel. What had Gideon said? Anything unexpected? So was I being paranoid? It was the right size for a book. And what else could it be that might be dangerous? How would George Smiley deal with it? He'd get someone from London Centre to check it for poison, or explosives, or ...

As soon as Hilary had finished her call, I rang Gideon.

'You just beat me to it. I was about to call you. Patterson.'

'You know what happened?'

'Of course. I was there.'

'I didn't see you.'

'But I saw you. And heard you.'

'Heard me?'

'Sure. Errol had a mike trained on you.'

'Ah. False alarm then.'

'That happens. Better to be safe than sorry.'

'Well, now you say that...' I told him about the uninvited parcel.

'Hmm. It's probably OK. Not the sort of thing I'd expect our Cambridge man to do. Still ... give it to Errol to check.'

'I'll do it later, when Hilary's out. I think she said she's got to get some cat food. ... Er, how will you check?

'We've got some equipment not far away. At the RAF base. We'll have it back to you in no time - if there's no problem.'

RAF Valley is just a couple of miles outside Holyhead, but the roads are a bit winding. It would take Errol/Eryl ten or fifteen minutes to get there. And a similar time to get back - longer, if the ferry-boat traffic was building up. Plus time for the tests...

'Hilary is bound to be back before Errol. And I don't want her wondering what's going on.'

Gideon thought for a moment.

'You're going to have to adopt a subterfuge.'

'You mean tell a lie?'

'Just put another book on your desk, one that she doesn't know, then if she asks, you can say it was only a complimentary copy from someone.'

'She might not ask.'

'Well, there you are. Either way, you're covered. And when Errol gets back with the real book ...'

If it's a book .. and if he brings it back ...

' ... he can leave it somewhere safe, so you can pick it up when you're on your own.'

'Like where?'

'Oh, anywhere. You got a dustbin outside?'

'Of course.'

'He'll leave it inside.'

'Are you serious?'

'You got a better idea?'

I had to admit I hadn't.

'Right then. Keep me posted if anything else happens.'

'I will.' A thought struck me. 'But Gideon...'

'Yeah?'

'Has anything more happened at your end?'

His tone was abrupt. 'We're still working on it.' This was evidently none of my business. Then, as if he realized how he was sounding ... 'I'll give you another call tomorrow morning.'

Hilary went out around two, and I took the parcel out to Errol/Eryl straight away. He placed it carefully in a container. It was the shortest of exchanges. 'You're expecting this,' I said. 'I am,' he said.

As I thought, Hilary was back within the hour, and each time I looked outside, I could see 'Stan' pottering about, but that was all. No van. I didn't have to 'adopt my subterfuge'. Hilary asked casually about the parcel at one point and I gave a nondescript answer. Just a book from a colleague.

I must say it felt really weird, doing a surreptitious dustbin check at regular intervals, while we wrote our begging letters to the people in Patterson's list. And even weirder when, by the end of the evening, there was nothing in the bin that looked remotely like a book. I'd ask Gideon about it tomorrow. Enough excitement for one day. And Tuesday looked as if it was going to be calmer.

I've never been more wrong.

15

The team arrived as usual at around nine, and I spent an hour with them. Hilary had fixed up with the TV researcher to meet me at the Hut Circles at 11. She checked me over before I left. No buttons left undone. Tie straight. I left straight away. It was only a few minutes drive, but I like to be early for these things. It's a regular source of humour, in our family. Dad always leaves so early to catch a train that he ends up getting to the station in time to catch the one before.

The Circles are just off the road that leads up to South Stack. A very popular tourist spot in the summer, and even though it was early January there were several cars in the car park opposite the site. Bird watchers, I thought. Dog walkers as well. A minibus with a scout troop name on it. Day out for them. But not such a brilliant day. There was a sea-mist coming in. It can cover the mountain in no time at all. We often look out of our window at home and say 'No mountain today'. It completely vanishes from sight.

I crossed the road and pushed open the gate into the field. There's a stile too, but the last time I went that way I slipped on the top stone, and twisted an ankle, so I avoided it. A wide grassy path leads up to the main group of circles, separating swathes of bracken. There were more than fifty huts here originally, stretching from the modern road for several hundred yards up the slope towards the main mass of the mountain. Only about twenty can be seen now, lying above the cultivated fields that now cover their neighbours.

You get a real sense of an old community here. The archaeologists have detected signs of habitation going back several thousand years. The surviving huts were inhabited between the second and fourth centuries AD. The people chose their location well. If it's a windy day - as it usually is - when you enter the site, the wind suddenly drops, and it becomes eerily silent. They built the huts in the lee of the mountain, sheltered from the south-westerlies that power in from the Irish Sea. It's like going from a busy street into a church.

It was a clever location too. It's high enough up the mountain slopes to look east across the whole of Anglesey, with the Snowdon range thirty miles in the distance. If enemies were coming, they'd be easily seen. And there were many enemies in those days - first, the Romans, and then, after the Romans had established themselves, Irish pirates. The Romans were well aware of the threat. They built a fortress-protected port in Holyhead, and constructed a watchtower on the top of the mountain to give the troops some advance warning.

I threaded my way through the hut remains, imagining how it must have been. The buildings were scattered, without any obvious plan, though there are signs of an ancient roadway running through the settlement. I passed some small rectangular constructions - for storing grain, the archaeologists think, and at least one was found to have signs of metal-working - and reached the two big circular huts, with stone walls just three or four feet high. Two large stones mark an entrance, and opposite this is a large firestone. The walls should be higher, but many of the stones were taken away by farmers in earlier times to build their field boundary walls. There would have had conical roofs made of thatch or turf and supported by wooden poles. Long gone.

I sat myself down on the wall of my favourite hut - it's over twenty feet across, with the largest and best preserved firestone. At my feet, embedded in the soil, was a stone bowl - an old mortar, used for crushing grain. If anything represented the spirit of Celtic peoples, it was this place. But whoever lived here is a mystery. In Welsh, the site is now called 'Cytiau'r Gwyddelod' - Irishmen's huts - presumably because of a later association with Irish settlers, though nothing is known about them.

There was nobody there but me. I assumed the crew were filming up at South Stack and would be down soon. I looked at my watch. My imaginings had passed the time. It was just before eleven. They'd have to hurry. The mist was beginning to build up. In the distance I could see a plane taking off from RAF Valley. Pilots back at work after the New Year break. I wondered what had happened to my parcel.

A car arrived in the car park and a man got out. He looked around him, then stood by the car park entrance, staring up towards me. He crossed the road, climbed over the stile, and walked purposefully in my direction, looking up at me the whole time. I don't know what it was. Instinct? Premonition? This wasn't right. He didn't wave. A TV person would have waved. And he wasn't carrying any equipment. I felt scared. A chill swept through me. Was this what Gideon had been anticipating? I had to get back to my car, but there wasn't a way without going right past the man. Only one path led to the road.

I needed to find some people. Further up the hill there was a house where some friends had started a guest house. I could go there. They'd have a phone, and I could call Gideon. I left my hut and walked as fast as I could along the path, and clambered a few feet down into their back garden. I hammered on the door. No reply. I hammered again. Nothing. And the door was locked. I looked back along the path. The man had stopped by the first group of circles, but he was still looking in my direction.

I wondered if I could get back to the road from the house. Not a chance. It would take me right past the man. I had no alternative but to keep going up the path. I knew exactly where it went. It was one of the walking routes across the base of the mountain. If I followed it, it would take me to the Breakwater Park. The man probably wouldn't know that. At least, I hoped he wouldn't. There was definitely a phone in the museum. I'd seen it when waiting for Patterson.

I scrambled back up to the path. I felt like running, but the terrain wasn't in favour of that. It was uneven and uphill. And besides, I couldn't remember the last time I'd run anywhere. The closest I'd come to athletics was editing its entries. I looked back. The man had started up along the same path, but he was still some distance behind. Maybe he wasn't fit either.

And then, a stroke of luck. The boy scouts - the ones from the minibus, I assumed - came into view. They'd evidently been to the top of the mountain and were on their way back to the car park. They'd probably seen the sea-mist coming in. I had an idea. As I passed the scout leader, I told him there was a man who'd hurt his leg a couple of hundred yards back. Might they be able to help him? I pointed him out. The scouts were delighted. A real job to do.

I carried on up the path until it levelled out. I looked back. The eager scouts were clustered around the man, who I imagined was trying to persuade them there was nothing wrong with him. I was above the road into Holyhead now, and there were houses coming into view - the mountain village that used to be quarrymen's houses. I looked back again. My delaying tactic hadn't caused as much delay as I'd hoped. The figure of my follower was appearing at the top of the rise. He was about a quarter of a mile away. I could just about see him in the mist, which was beginning to swirl down the mountain. But that would leave me plenty of time to get down to the Park. It would soon be downhill, a bit steep, but not for too long. All I had to do was turn right after I passed the village. Keeping going on the same path would take me up over the top of the quarry towards North Stack.

I'm not sure to this day what happened. Maybe it was my panic. Or the mist, which had now reached my path. Sea-mist is like a thick white fog, only clammier. And it makes things look very different. But I suspect it was more the way the landscape had actually altered. The storms of the past few days had blown branches, bushes, and other stuff all over the place, and I think some of it had got onto the path just where it turned right, obscuring the turning. Whatever the reason, I missed it, and by the time I realized I'd gone wrong, it was too late to turn back. I would have to carry on towards North Stack, and come back down to the Park from there.

It was a trickier route, and much more dangerous, especially in the mist. An old path branched right. It took you straight to the top of the cliffs - presumably from the days before that part of the mountain had been blasted away. I knew it, from the days when I'd had the ambition to walk every path on the mountain - and succeeded. I'd gone a few yards up the old path, seen the cliff edge right in front of me, hidden by the gorse, and turned back just in time. The gorse spills over the edge, and the path suddenly falls away beneath your feet. I grabbed the gorse to steady myself. I wasn't wearing gloves. It took me days to get all the splinters out of my hands.

I went past the old path, but a few yards on I found my way blocked by another wind-blown bush. This time it was a blessing. I pulled it back down to the junction so that it spread across the main path. With luck, the man would follow the old path, realize his mistake, and turn back to look for me further down. I scuttled back up the hill and hid behind a large rock. Visibility was down to just a few yards now.

The plan almost worked. I heard him come up the hill, very much out of breath. He followed the old path, as I'd hoped. And when he got to the top, just as I'd thought, he stopped and turned round. The bit I hadn't anticipated was the angle of vision. I'd placed myself behind the rock so that I couldn't be seen from the main pathway. I'd forgotten that, as the old path went up to the cliff top, it bent to the left, so that at the top, when he turned round, he could see where I was, crouching there, even in the mist. I could see him reaching into his jacket and pulling out a gun. I shut my eyes and prayed. There was a shot.

I opened my eyes and he had disappeared. A voice said, 'Are you OK?'

It was Gideon.

16

'I'm really sorry. That sort of thing shouldn't happen.'

We were in Gideon's car, on our way back to where I'd left mine. I was still shaking. My jacket and trousers were a total mess. Heaven knows what Hilary would say.

'How - how - ' I found I couldn't talk.

'Take it easy. You're in shock. Here.' He reached into the glove compartment and pulled out a bottle of brandy. 'Take a good swig.' I did.

'How did you find me.'

'I called your house just after you left, and your wife told me where you were. Why didn't you tell me where you were going? I warned you.'

'I didn't think it was important. You said I was to tell you if something unexpected happened. But calls from the BBC aren't anything out of the ordinary. This was routine.'

'Except this one wasn't. I called our man at the BBC and he checked. It only took him a few minutes to establish that there was no such programme being filmed up here today.'

We reached the car park. The mist swirled around the car.

'I don't think I can drive', I said. 'I'm just too shaky.'

'It doesn't matter. Arthur will drive you home.'

'Arthur?'

'Sure. You've seen him by your house.'

'Oh, Stan.'

'Huh? Who?'

'Nothing. Sorry. Feeling a bit muddled.'

Gideon switched off the engine. 'It was just as well you left early. It gave us the time we needed to get everyone in place.'

'Sorry. I'm not with you. What do you mean, in place?'

'I sent Errol and Arthur to the Hut Circles to get you, while I waited near your place. When they couldn't find you, they asked some people whether they'd seen you. Some scouts said they'd seen two men on the lower mountain path. Errol called me and I went straight to the Park path to intercept you.'

'How did you know your way?'

'What do you think I was doing all day Saturday, when I passed you near the Park? I wanted to be sure I had all escape routes planned in case we got into trouble with dear Mr Patterson. I now know this side of the mountain as well as you do. Well, almost.'

'What's happened to the man who was after me?'

'I had to take him out.'

'Where is he?'

'In the quarry. I've sent Errol to clear up the mess. All I'm hoping is that the fall wasn't seen. Probably wouldn't be, in this mist. I don't want the local rescue services around. It would only complicate things.'

'You're being very ... ' I searched for a word. ' ... casual about all this, Gideon.'

Gideon grinned. 'All part of the job. This isn't the first time I've had to deal with hitmen. And actually, David, I'm quite impressed with you.'

'Why on earth?'

'Well some targets get very emotional when they've been through a situation like this. I wouldn't blame you if you were in tears.'

I managed a weak smile. That would come later, I expected.

'But tell me. How did our man end up going so near the cliff edge?'

I explained my ruse with the bush. Gideon grabbed my shoulder in delight. 'Now I'm even more impressed. We could do with men like you in the service. Want a job?'

'I'll stick to editing, thanks.'

I looked down at my torn and dirty clothes. 'What am I going to tell Hilary?'

'The truth, if you want to. As long as she signs one of our secrecy forms.'

'Really? Is this thing over?'

'Almost. Just one more small job to do.'

Gideon saw my face change, and added hurriedly. 'But don't worry. There's no danger now. As soon as their hitman fails to report, they'll know we're onto them, and they'll pull the operation. And just to make sure, we'll use our system to let them know.'

'How do you mean?'

'We'll send a message to all the countries telling them the Feb meeting has been cancelled, and not to expect any further contact. They'll know what that means.' He opened the car door, and began to get out, then turned back. 'And when I say "we", I mean "you". Then I think we're done.'

'How will I know what to say?'

'I'll tell you. And it has to be today. I'll call at your place later, after I've caught up with Errol.' He grinned. 'And after you've had a chance to explain your torn jacket to Hilary.'

He went over to talk to Arthur, who was standing by his van. The BT logo looked quite dramatic through the mist. After a few minutes he came back and opened my door.

'I'm going over to the Park with the van to meet Errol and, er ... to pick stuff up. Have you got your keys?'

Oh yes, my car keys. I handed them to Arthur. 'You all right?' he asked. 'I've been better,' I replied.

We were home five minutes later. I looked at my watch. It was two o'clock. I realized I was feeling very hungry.

Arthur parked my car in the drive and went into his roadworks hut. 'Take it easy, now,' he said laconically. Not a man of many words.

Hilary was downstairs, and came to the front door when she heard the car.

'That took a while,' she said. 'You wouldn't think a TV int- '

She looked at my jacket. Then my trousers.

'I can explain,' I said weakly.

'I hope so.' I went into the house. 'And while you're at it, can you tell me how a brand-new copy of the Japanese translation of the *Cambridge Encyclopedia of Language* ended up in our dustbin?'

17

It took an hour to tell the whole story. I played down the drama of the last hour or so, and indeed have never told anyone the full story until now. Halfway through, Gideon arrived. 'The marketing man,' Hilary observed wryly, as she signed the Official Secrets Act. I was amazed at how calm she was.

Gideon continued to be professional. He warned us about the shock we would continue to feel, and offered counselling if we needed it. It wasn't an offer we ever took up. Indeed, looking back, I find it difficult to believe how equable we both were. The worst that happened was the odd nightmare or vivid dream. The whole thing felt unreal, surreal. It still does.

'We need to get this message off pronto.'

'What do you want me to say?'

'Simply tell them that the next meeting has been cancelled, and that the Cambridge link is no more. I don't mind the exact wording.'

'It'll depend on what I can find in the listings.'

"Will it take long? If not, I'll wait.'

'Shouldn't be. I'll use the listing I did for Armenia, remember?'

'Ah yes, the Crystal meeting.'

'That's half the job done.'

And it didn't take long, thanks to Hilary volunteering to help with the counting. I ended up with this set of substitutions and locations:

59	cancelled	C04
60	keeper	K03
61	news	N03
63	talks	T02
77	latest	L04
86	warning	W03
93	urgency	U11
98	coalition	C15
102	liquidated	L09
107	uncovered	U01

'How's about this? It's a bit wordy, but I had to use all the word changes in the entry, and there were quite a few in Armenia.' I showed him my screen with the message I'd put together:

news urgency warning
latest talks cancelled
keeper uncovered
coalition liquidated

Gideon gave me a thumbs-up. 'Splendid. And the code?'

I scrolled down.

'Armenia N03U11W03L04T02C04K03U01C15L09. Who'll send it?'

'Our man in Cambridge. Let me copy it down and I'll phone it through.'

'When you say "our man..." '

Gideon grinned. 'I mean OUR man.'

'And the mole?'

'He's ... shall we say, not working at Cambridge any more, since this morning. In fact there's a vacancy in the printing house, if you're interested?'

I didn't ask what had happened to him. Nor did I ask, as we walked outside, what was in the back of Errol/Eryl's van, along with the tent and other equipment that he and Arthur were putting away.

Just outside the front door, Gideon stopped. 'Oh, I almost forgot. I'll need a copy of the printout of the files. For the archive.'

I went upstairs and put the pile of papers into a large jiffy bag, and passed them over. As we stood at our front gate, Gideon turned to Hilary and me. ' Call me if you need to.'

A thought occurred to me. 'While I remember... I'm due to give a talk at the Royal Institution next month about the Encyclopedia. Can I tell any of this there?'

'You can talk about the changes up to your CIS entry, but nothing after that.'

'Not ever?'

'Well, not for 25 years, or until the Home Office decides otherwise.'

'What then?'

'Take a leaf out of Le Carré's books. Tell it as a story. Add a bit of fiction. Change the names. You might make your fortune.'

'Hmm.' Hilary and I looked at each other. She got in first with what we were both thinking. 'Encyclopedia editing won't, that's for sure.'

'But if you do write something, don't use the exact codes that we discovered. replace them with something similar - and shorter. Just to be on the safe side.'

I couldn't imagine what that might mean, but Gideon was warming to his theme. 'You could even say you were responsible for the final break-up of the Soviet Union.'

'Me?'

'Well, without your input we would never have cracked that code. Next month's meeting would have gone ahead, and who knows what catastrophes would have followed from it! At least three assassinations were being planned. There could have been more.' He got into his car.

Arthur and Stan finished putting the last of the roadwork materials into the van, and drove off, without a word. Gideon wound down his car window.

'And it would make a great opening line for a novel'.

That was the last I saw of him - apart from once. He was sitting in the back row at my Royal Institution talk a few weeks later. When I told my story about the Commonwealth of Independent States, I could see him smiling, and he gave me a silent clap at the end of it. There was real applause when I finished the lecture, but it's his silent acknowledging gesture that has always stayed with me.

Appendix

In this appendix I reproduce extracts from the word-lists used by the Cambridge mole and by me when responding. Unfortunately, I'm not allowed to publish the complete lists, which I suppose are now somewhere in a Home Office archive; but in any case the originals were extremely long: the printout of all the different words in the Cambridge Encyclopedia amounted to nearly 90,000 items, and included thousands of personal and historical names. Gideon did however give me permission to present an abridged form of the original listings, so I've included the lists for all of the 30 numerical values used in my narrative, but showing only the everyday words that would be found in a general English dictionary, along with a selection of place names (all uncapitalized). This should be enough for anyone who might wish to get a sense of the scale and originality of the enterprise devised by the Cambridge agent. In my narrative I've recalculated the locational codes to tie in with this abridgement.

Anyone wishing to add further words to these lists for their own purposes, using the same system (A = 1 to Z = 26), may of course do so, and these days the task will be aided by several online sites that provide automatic calculations of word totals. All one has to do is type 'gematria calculator' into a search engine.

Value 31
alabama, ask, bann, based, bath, beads, bees, bell, bias, bit, bleach, bleak, blob, canal, cared, cash, cave, cedar, chief, cine, cis, cnn, coal, coded, cola, cube, damage, danced, debt, demi, dime, echo, fall, fax, gabled, gagged, gain, garda, gear, gene, ghana, hard, heeded, her, hick, hub, ideal, lame, land, male, meal, mr, nap, nice, nob, old, op, pack, pan, raced, rage, rid, safe

Value 32
aachen, academe, adder, again, agenda, ages, aimed, arabia, arcade, arid, arm, bait, ballad, barbed, bark, beagle, beet, bench, bloc, bomb, boo, bye, cased, cell, chat, cheek, cock, coma, con, damn, dared, dash, decked, deer, dew, dine, dread, dug, nded, eve, facial, fate, feat, file, gall, get, hare, hear, high, jail, jeddah, jihad, label, lane, lean, life, load, madam, mar, media, men, mod, ms, pig, rabbi, raid, ram, reed, sage, she, tic, uk, via, wed

Value 52
abused, academy, accuse, adorn, adverb, african, ailing, alibis, aligned, altar, amino, antacid, arcing, argue, arise, arran, ashes, auks, avon, awash, ballet, bananas, barbell, barcoded, bargain, barges, barrage, basing, baton, batted, baykal, besiege, binder, bioko, birds, blimp, blocked, blonde, blow, booked, boot, bowl, braved, byte, cadets, calcified, calmer, camps, canker, caring, catalan, cavalcade, ceases, celtic,

ceramic, charmed, chilean, clashed, cleaved, coding, combs, copied, corgi, create, crop, cudgel, curia, dakota, daleks, dancing, dealing, debatable, debut, declared, decline, decoy, defected, deter, devil, dijon, docks, dodoma, dons, door, dryad, dwarf, dyer, earth, eaves, ejected, elegance, enacted, epics, erased, farces, fareham, felon, felted, fences, finance, finds, finer, finned, fiord, firs, flood, flora, fluid, fodder, forage, form, freer, friar, from, funk, gates, giraffe, ging, golem, gorge, graft, grange, graz, grime, grind, gull, halls, halved, handy, harbin, hater, hazel, heart, hello, herbs, hips, hobby, ills, impala, impede, inbred, indiana, infer, jamaican, jobber, kept, kilt, kiwi, last, leading, legible, lived, loud, malay, manes, manx, marched, marked, mart, mass, means, merged, modena, names, necks, negate, nova, now, official, omani, own, paler, patna, peaks, pearl, perm, plain, pong, pope, pride, rabbit, racing, radon, raise, ramadan, refer, reno, riddle, rink, rite, rubbed, rum, salsa, salt, sandbach, seeds, seine, sendai, shall, ship, shy, sill, sinai, six, skim, slaked, sledge, sliced, some, speak, spice, staff, stage, tackle, tended, thaw, thigh, tier, tire, traded, tram, triad, udder, vamp, weigh, well, what, whiff, wit, won, zambia, zebra, zinc

Value 53

accorded, achieve, adduct, aerobic, affirm, aiming, airy, albino, algeria, aloud, amass, amenable, anaconda, apaches, archer, atlas, attach, attic, aural, axis, backbone, bahrain, ballgame, bandages, barmen, beaver, bedknob, begonia, bigot, biogas, blackleg, blockade, blur, bohemia, bongo, boogie, boreal, bough, brained, bramble, breeds, brill, calcite, camels, carbon, carved, casing, casks, caused, cdrom, chances, checker, chelsea, chicano, chicken, chicks, chilled, choir, cinder, clocked, clogged, cloned, cobalt, coerced, coffin, colds, comeback, conceal, conceded, cooked, coombe, coot, copra, cowl, craved, craze, cupid, curbed, dagenham, dampen, damps, daphnia, daring, darken, database, debauched, deceive, deeper, depth, detain, diabetic, diagram, didactic, disband, divide, drop, dundee, dyes, eczema, emerge, endemic, ending, escaped, ethane, exact, fairs, farcical, fecund, fines, fjord, flanked, frigid, ganges, gender, gerbil, glum, goggle, graces, grave, grew, guild, guy, hacking, hanger, haste, heats, hoofed, hues, hull, hyena, iguana, inhaled, inks, jacaranda, jackdaw, jains, jaws, killed, knew, labelled, lapse, leaches, leaps, legacy, lieder, lineage, lineal, lobes, logs, look, machine, maharaja, malaya, mammal, manacled, many, masked, mast, mats, meant, medlar, menu, mirage, monk, moped, needy, niger, nose, oars, oldham, ones, pacified, paired, phased, phobic, pith, pleas, pledged, ponce, puke, pup, quack, quebec, ramat, ranked, ready, reefs, regalia, regard, reign, relied, remake, repaid, ricin, rift, rioja, rot, run, sabbath, sacks, scenic, scheme, seaman, shank, shaped, sheep, silage, silica, sink, site, skin, slabs, slang, sledded, slim, soar, sos, spied, stabbed, steed, sum, taboo, tacit, talked, tarn, ties, till, tome, tor, track, udine, urn, usage, vicar, vigo, vocal, vodka, wafer, wait, welded, wheel, whim, wield, wing, wipe, womb, woo, wye, yew, yucca

Value 59
abbots, abkhazia, ablest, about, accessed, accident, accreted, adsorb, afforded, akron, alaskan, alberta, almond, amphibia, amuse, anchor, andante, annelid, arachnida, ararat, arnhem, aryan, avarice, average, backers, bacteria, badajoz, baleful, bandaging, barbels, barnes, beacons, beggars, behest, belize, bellman, bicycle, binding, biplane, biscay, bison, bloated, blues, boards, boers, booby, bores, bows, braille, brass, breathe, brechin, brent, briefs, broaden, broads, buddhas, buddleja, budget, buried, burr, calcify, calming, canasta, cancelled, canonic, cartel, cashew, casket, catches, ceiling, celts, chambered, chaotic, charted, chateau, cheque, cipher, civet, claret, cleanse, clips, college, colon, comrade, coolie, copy, cords, couched, creams, credit, crimp, crow, cruel, cups, cusp, datum, decency, decibels, decrees, defiant, delegate, delicate, devoid, dimple, direct, dives, docetic, dogmas, donate, double, dragon, drainage, dubbing, dying, educate, eltham, emanate, embarked, embolic, endive, etcher, ethnic, euro, evict, exiled, exude, fairy, fallible, feasible, ferric, fescue, fibres, films, finger, fining, foods, forked, fort, fringe, gardenia, gather, genome,

gills, goblin, gouged, gown, greased, gyri, habits, hamlet, hardened, harms, hating, hazes, hedgehog, heirs, hexham, holes, husk, idols, imphal, income, infield, inky, invaded, ipanema, island, jumna, kindled, kits, koalas, koran, krona, lahore, lairs, laramie, larvae, lasagne, launch, leaching, leaking, learned, leaseback, lemon, liberal, liberica, limped, linear, lines, linkage, logical, loire, malawi, maldon, manager, manatee, marred, marsh, melon, melted, mimes, minds, minehead, miner, molar, moral, moved, muddle, mumbai, munch, mute, negro, nomadic, null, oases, offended, offered, opened, oxfam, pacts, pains, pavane, pears, pedalled, pencil, perched, pidgin, pinched, pint, posed, pupae, radish, rails, reaches, recedes, rectal, reddened, redeemed, reels, robes, rook, ruanda, scales, scream, sedges, seeing, seeks, shire, sickle, sidecar, size, skaldic, skit, slash, slave, slew, slug, sober, social, solid, soy, spacelab, spain, spare, spear, stable, sudan, swap, tables, taliban, tangle, tart, tenable, tent, theft, third, tiger, tinged, toads, tobacco, toes, toll, twig, ulcer, umber, varied, veered, veined, view, vigil, viola, wakes, wasp, weaken, weird, whelk, where, whom, wider, winded, wired, wish, yalta, yeti, yogic, zagreb, zaire

Value 60
abandoned, abducted, academies, acouchi, acrobat, active, addicts, adheres, advise, affairs, affects, airmen, aliens, allot, amirs, amlwch,

amoral, animalia, annelida, anobiidae, apium, appealed, apses, araucana, arborea, arching, ascetic, ashram, asilidae, atoll, attar, avoided, balkans, banjul, barnet, basenji, bashing, battle, bedstead, believe, bengals, berlin, bielefeld, billy, blazar, blinds, blotch, bogota, bolls, bonsai, booth, borax, bosnia, bounce, breaker, buckden, buffet, busied, byname, cagliari, cameras, cantata, canvas, caravan, carlsbad, carrara, castle, cathedra, caught, celibacy, cement, chafers, chalky, chariclea, charing, checking, chichewa, cinclidae, cithara, clavata, clays, clues, coachella, coaching, codename, coins, coital, coley, collide, confided, cores, cows, cranes, cubans, cumin, cushi, cycladic, darner, decrease, defeats, demands, depot, desire, detailed, devon, diamond, diocese, discalced, dracula, dragger, drawn, dreams, dukes, dunbar, durban, eclectic, edicts, edifices, elint, enticed, epee, epochal, ercilla, erected, errand, etches, expo, eyelid, fallacy, fault, fearing, ferghana, fiesta, finland, flaking, flapped, flung, forli, fossa, found, four, freaks, fugue, funen, gadwall, gauges, gauls, gauze, gdynia, geckos, gerona, ginger, glendale, globes, gonads, goods, gorki, gouache, grading, graffham, grant, guarded, gums, habilis, habitable, hadron, haloes, halts, hangings, happen, headers, hearth, hectare, helps, hendon, heraldic, heron, hiccup, hills, hinted, hobbies, holy, homes, hotel, hutch, hymn, icelandic, icons, imaging, imbalance, incite, indies, induced, inedible, inflame, inlet, inner, inside, intake, intel, jilted, jokes, judical, jump, karoo, kauri, keeper, keys, kildare, kings, knot, laccadive, lacecaps, lakeland, lancing, lapland, likened, list, loans, located, locks, loran, luganda, luggage, lured, lush, lyre, magnet, malaise, manages, mandible, marine, maxim, menaces, mews, mines, minilab, minx, miss, morn, mosaic, mugs, nebulae, nimes, norm, notch, occur, often, opted, orange, order, ouse, over, paddler, paint, panicle, papaya, pelican, peril, peru, pest, pets, pickled, pierced, pikes, pips, police, pomp, porch, pork, pray, preached, preceded, probed, pure, quail, raking, rarer, raven, recalled, reduced, regicide, relax, rely, remain, renamed, replace, resale, reside, retake, rhone, ribbon, ridgeback, robbef, rove, rubs, ruled, rung, sails, saipan, saline, scaly, scanned, scars, score, scaler, second, sept, sewage, shams, sheared, sheikh, shekel, shellac, sieve, silt, sisal, skye, sleigh, slit, smash, soft, sonic, soya, spike, spy, staked, step, stiff, succeed, tablet, taipei, takaoka, taper, tariff, teacher, thatch, their, tobago, tote, toy, trail, trial, trim, tune, twice, uncial, usable, valet, verbal, ashrama,vexed, vow, wagon, waive, wales, warhead, washed, weals, whit, with, word, wreck, wren, yoked, yuma, zaandam, zone

Value 61

amiens, amiss, anglican, angst, anjou, annals, anthem, argot, armenia, ascribed, asking, atomic, avocado, axles, babblers, baneful, bangkok, banjaxed, banning, bargained, barricade, bathing, beakers, beatified, bedchamber, befits, benefit, benthic, bergamo, berried, birdman, biting, blackadder, blackcock, bleaching, bliss, blondie, bogside, boiler, boney, booted, borate, bowled, boyne, boys, breaches, breeze, bribing, broadband, brook, budding, bumped, calculi, caloric, candelabra, candidate, cannock, cannon, canter, carbides, carefree, carts, cascading, casino, cattle, cents, charcoal, charges, chasing, chiffon, chipped, chordal, chubby, church, clause, coarse, coimbra, collar, combine, coming, confer, creeks, cyanide, dalliance, dalmatia, damming, danzig, daoism, dative, datong, davos, deacons, decoding, defences, defender, deform, deltas, detachable, dieter, dipole, dredger, drenched, droll, duchy, duels, dwarfed, early, earthed, easels, ebony, echoing, elegiacs, eligible, emaciated, embargo, encamped, endow, entail, eureka, falkland, falling, farmer, farnham, females, finals, fives, flares, flaws, flint, flooded, foils, formed, fractal, franer, francs, fujian, fulham, fungal, gaining, gallon, gamelin, gannet, gearing, generic, gifts, girder, giver, gladly, glances, glencoe, glove, gnarled, gnats, goblet, goose, grafted, grasp, grazed, guise, guns, habitat, hairy, halifax, having, hearted, heathen, heaths, heavy, hebrew, hoods, humble, hums, hyoid, inject, inlay, jumbo, kalahari, kasbahs, kennel, kinder, knobs, lambeth, lamps, landing, laoise, larger, larks, lasted, layer, leaflet, leakages, leases, legacies, linz, litchi, loans, lodger, loos, macaque, magenta, magnate, magus, maharajah, majorca, mallard, manageable, manor, massed, maths, meadow, mediated, megohm, melodic, mendip, meter, metre, milder, miracle, mist, monaco, mons, moor, morbid, mynah, navaho, nectar, news, niigata, ningbo, obtain, ocarina, official, oily, ooze, ordain, oslo, owned, packing, paddles, palms, pasadena, paste, patio, pays, pebbles, phallic, phlegm, piles, pleader, prime, psalm, pull, quick, quin, radars, rains, rallied, rebels, recant, reclaim, refined, reject, relate, relay, ribbing, richer, riding, roman, room, rwanda, salon, salted, sander, scampi, scent, screech, seems, sends, setback, sewn, sheath, shone, sins, sleet, sling, smell, smock, solo, spate, staffed, stele, sung, sync, tabasco, tails, taipan, tannic, tapes, teaches, thawed, tiered, tilt, tonic, took, tralee, trance, trendtrick, urbane, vacant, value, vanes, vent, verged, waging, wands, warble, wars, weighed, wimp, wore, wow, yankee, you

Value 63
academician, accolades, accords, acetone, adherence, agencies, agitate, airmail, allow, animate, annual, appease, applied, array, asians, asses, atonal, avatar, averaged, awaited, awful, backward, balancing, barely, basking, besides, biofeedback, biomes, blasted, boxcar, bracts, brains, bravado, breathed, bridgehead, bridgend, broader, broom, bubbles, buffalo, burial, butane, butt, calorie, camping, cancers, cannabis, carbolic, cardioid, carmine, carpet, caspian,

catnip, cavern, cereals, chaconne, changing, chiefdom, chinese, chitin, ciliated, classed, clerical, client, climate, clinical, clocks, coalesce, color, combated, combing,command, concave, conics, cooks, corfu, cover, cracow, craven, creaky, crimean, crowd, curled, cuts, degrees, deity, delegated, demonic, denote, derive, descended, detainee, deviance, diagonal, dimly, dimpled, discoid, divine, docking, dolmen, donated, doubled, drawback, dumped, dunes, durable, dutied, earwig, educated, elders, eleven, elves, emanated, embedding, equable, erasable, exuded, factor, faiths, familial, fantail, feather, femur, fiery, finding, finite, firing, fisted, fixes, flagging, flanks, flashback, floated, flux, folks, freesia, friday, fringed, frolic, fuels, gallop, garner, gaunt, genetic, gentle, gimbals, ginkgo, godly, golfer, gout, gozo, groin, grow, handles, hardier, harebell, helmet, herbicide, highland, hives, hopes, hunt, incapable, inchon, incised, indebted, indices, inhabit, innate, ireland, irish, jazz, jinhua, kills, knocked, know, krone, ladders, lebanese, lebanon, legume, libyan, liffey, limit, limpid, lough, maggot, mainz, malleable, mallet, manakin, maracaibo, masks, matted, meaning, mermaid, meuse, minder, mislead, motif, muddled, muon, muted, nagasaki, nagoya, namibian, napier, next, nigeria, noone, nordic, nudes, oasis, oaths, obscene, octet, odessa, offices, olive, opals, optic, packages, pagodas, pairs, palatal, panicked, paris, parsed, paunch, peaking, peers, penis, pescara, pines, pixie, played, pleated, plot, pluck, pouch, public, racism, ranger, ranks, rates, ratio, rays, reaper, rebelled, record, regained, remedied, remind, reveal, rhyl, roofed, ruse, saddler, saint, samoan, sandy, sanicle, satin, scrub, seamy, searched, seeding, seeker, senegal, serbs, sets, shackled, shakes, siberia, sifted, sight, sized, skies, skill, smoke, sniffed, snipe, soccer, soons, spaces, spared, spine, spread, spree. stacked, stain, stalk, stare, sucked, sure, swat, tabloid, talks, tangled, tears, teens, tense, tint, tirana, topic, traffic, trip, try, user, veldt, visage, weaker, wedges, weeks, whole, wiggle, witch, yarra, yolk, yule

Value 64
advised, airfield, alarms, almanacs, ambient, ambush, american, angers, angling, angolan, aniline, apron, arrange, arty, aspect, asset, attend, audited, awakened, azov, bachelor, baldness, bailiffs, balletic, barium, barter, basins, battled, bayou, believed, belonged, benares, bermuda, bicameral, birches, birdland, blackmail, blinder, bombarded, boolean, booms, boron, bosom, bossed, botanic, bounced, boxer, brandy, breeding, bridges, bright, brimmed, bubbly, built, burden, burned, cadmium, campaign, candidacy, captain, carcass, cerebral, chapels, chaplain, cheery, cheeses, chianti, chosen, chums, churn, cinemas, cinerama, clings, clouded, cobbling, codfish, cogent, coiner, collided, comedian, commas, compel, condom, cools, coping, coward, cress, czechs, damping, dancers, dealers,

debtor, decimated, decreased, deflected, denials, depart, depose, desired, devise, diarrhea, digest, dinner, disarm, dishes, dockland, dover, dozen, dreamer, drilled, drove, dust, dwelt, dyeing, dykes, effects, elects, elegant, embody, enabling, encoder, engaging, enrol, ensue, epidemic, ermine, ethics, expand, factual, faroes, federate, filly, finches, fitted, flicker, floral, florid, fluidic, flute, focus, forfar, formic, forte, freckled, freeing, frisbee, fumes, funds, furs, gazing, glacials, glues, gorse, gradual, grass, greedy, greeted, guidance, gushed, hassle, haunt, heating, helper, hippo, hissed, hobart, horned, hypo, ignite, ilford, impeached, incited, infant, inflamed, inking, intifada, isles, isobar, israel, jackass, jelly, jubilee, kicking, kinks, kites, knoll, korean, lagoon, lawman, lazy, leaders, leaping, leaves, levy, litre, lobbies, loomed, maidenhead, marbella, mating, mazes, meaty, medley, melilla, mercy, michigan, milks, mingled, mohair, moles, mombasa, morale, movie, musk, needles, nerve, never, noun, nuclei, objected, oilman, onto, orbit, pageant, parades, parted, passed, paths, peebles, picket, piggy, piper, pits, plebeian, pocks, poise, polled, poor, prey, punjab, push, pyre, quay, racers, rafts, rainham, ranges, rateable, rearmed, recited, reliable, render, replaced, replica, resided, rhino, rhondda, sabres, sacking, saddles, sailer, saliva, says, sciatic, scored, screen, seats, seize, select, senate, senile, serial, shales, sieges, spades, spell, spiked, spit, stall, stud, succeeded, surf, swabs, swim, taming, tapir, tatami, tenet, test, thumb, tight, tips, torch, tray, treacle, treat, triadic, true, tucked, tuned, unit, uses, vehicle, vital, waived, warmed, watched, watt, widened, width, wilt, yielded, zero

Value 65
aborted, absurd, abundance, accents, admirable, adopted, adriatic, aerials, ainsdale, aisles, alerted, alicante, alkaline, alkalis, alloy, alphabet, altered, amnesiac, android, angry, appended, armies, assay, attacked, attain, available, azaleas, backyard, bagatelle, bakelite, bankside, barbers, basque, basses, bastard, beersheba, beguiled, belfast, beloved, beverage, beyond, billing, birdlife, bishkek, blackish, bladders, blanket, bonding, boring, boson, bounded, boxes, brahmin, breast, breeches, brigades, broken, bucolic, bulks, calyx, canines, carbonic, carry, carter, catching, centre, centre, chandler, chants, chaplet, choose, cities, cleaning, clefts, clever, clipped, clump, coaxial, cochlear, cocoon, cognate, combined, comedy, cougar, cowes, crater, creamy, crest, crevice, crisp, cupped, dactyl, darling, dearly, deference, deferred, delight, denser, describe, diabetes, diaries, distaff, diving, doping, doves, drains, draws, dress, durham, either, eldest, encodes, engulf, ergot, espy, exceeds, excise, fanning, farmhand, fasts, felling, ferried, fideism, fifteen, filmy, finish, fireball, firms, fisher, flammable, florida,flowed, footed, fordham, formal, freebased, freeze, frogs, fuelled, funchal, gambling, geelong, girls, gloved,

gory, gourd, gravel, greeks, guides, gulfs, gunned, haggling, hansard, hatchet, hatfield, headwear, heather, herbals, herding, highgate, hiring, horse, humbled, idiocy, imbibing, incur, indexed, indicate, ingot, islet, itchy, jailbird, jargon, kansas, kernel, kilns, kindred, lament, latvia, layby, lending, licking, lighted, lining, links, loss, loyal, macedonia, madrigal, maidens, mailing, malts, manly, manner, mantle, margate, massage, mastic, mayhem, medium, mekong, mental, merit, method, microbe, midst, mills, minted, mitre, modified, motel, mould, mown, mural, murcia, music, nearby, newer, ninth, oblong, offaly, orifice, ovoid, palpable, pandemic, parks, pasted, phials, phonic, pincer, pipes, pitched, poker, primed, prince, prop, pulp, pyx, rampaged, random, reaching, rebus, receding, recent, recur, reigate, reins, related, release, remit, renew, repay, repeat, resin, retail, risen, riyadh, rowed, rugs, ruhr, runic, rupee, sadism, saigon, salamanca, saver, scaling, scenes, sciatica, seaboard, seafood, sender, seven, sharjah, shelled, shocked, shore, show, sinned, siren, slum, smeared, snatch, solar, somme, spark, special, spey, stank, state, stay, steep, stile, suet, sunk, swami, tackng, taejon, tanks, tapioca, taste, teasable, teats, termed, threaded, tiles, today, token, tracer, treadle, turf, twang, tzar, ugly, unease, unpaid, upbeat, valued, vienna, waking, wander, warden, wards, warned, weasel, wends, white, willed, wiis, wool, wracked

Value 73
abrogated, abusing, accelerate, adhesive, adjunct, affiliated, affluence, agouti, albanians, aligning, alleluia, allocated, alnwick, amphibian, antigua, arachnoid, arbiter, around, arrive, aseptic, attachable, attended, avidly, axons, babirusa, backbenches, bangladesh, banners, barracks, bartered, bathers, batting, bellboy, besancon, bespoke, bexley, bighorn, billion, biomedical, bipolar, bivalve, bivouac, blackmailed, blocking, bloody, bluebird, booking, bought, brigadier, britain, bronx, broods, buckles, bulldog, cabinets, cadavers, cadenzas, campaigned, campus, captained, captor, carries, casting, central, cervical, chandigarh, charming, charter, chemicals, childlike, children, churned, circus, cirque, claimant, clashing, cleaving, climactic, closes, coalfish, coccyx, cockchafer, combat, comedies, comers, commit, common, compile, copper, corner, cortege, coughs, count, cowered, crafty, crazy, crises, croup, crown, crucible, crutch, curved, cuticle, cycling, cynics, deadlines, dearness, decalogue, declaring, defecting, efendant, defunct, denting, departed, descends, desiccated, detente, dialects, digested, disarmed, disliked, displaced, doggerel, dormer, dowager, driers, dukedom, dumps, during, dusted, eagerly, eclipsed, egypt, eighteen, ejecting, enacting, encircled, enclose, engines, episode, equated, erasing, escapades, evesham, except, expanded, expect, eyepiece, fainter, fatigued, fellow, fermanagh, ferrate, fighter, filofax, finest,

fishmeal, fists, floats, flying, focused, foresee, format, forum, fragrance, freehold, freelanced, freight, front, futile, gelatine, geologic, glaucoma, gneiss, gnomes, goddess, goodbye, graceful, gravy, greenleaf, grenades, grits, grodno, gudgeon, hairlike, haler, halibut, halving, happier, hasty, hateful, haunted, hawking, headless, heathland, heritage, hermit, herself, hoops, hunger, hydride, hygiene, impinge, infest, inflict, intuit, invader, iraqis, israeli, italics, javelin, kelvin, kettle, kingdom, knocks, kurds, labrus, landers, landlady, langur, larvik, latrobe, learner, lemming, lenoir, levite, leyland, linens, living, llanfair, lomond, loris, loves, lower, lungs, lwow, marching, marking, maximal, mayfair, meerkat, meeting, memoir, merging, meridian, migrate, militia, milkman, minorca, missal, motet, mouse, mover, muscle, must, naming, nantes, nation, navigable, nitric, normal, notes, number, obeisance, obelisk, occident, odour, offences, offender, onset, oracles, orbited, orgasm, orgies, ornate, ours, outback, pacemaker, packers, palsy, paperback, paradise, pastel, patchy, patience, pawns, peacocks, pelote, peopled, perfect, petals, petered, piccolo, pincher, pirated, planing, planks, plates, plays, pleura, poaching, polemic, pores, prefaces, prefect, preheat, preyed, prose, pulse, punjabi, pushed, quaker, quiz, ragtime, rainfall, rapeseed, rarebit, rasps, ravages, rayon, realised, really, recency, redeemer, regret, relearn, rendered, reopen, resold, revere, rhymed, riders, roast, roofs, rookie, ropes, rouble, rouen, rubbing, rugby, sacrifice, sausage, saxon, scandals, scapula, scramble, screened, seaplane, searing, season, secluded, selected, seminal, served, sexy, shafts, shaver, shrew, shrine, sidereal, sincere, slander, slavs, smogs, smut, socket, solder, solve, sound, sour, spadix, spanned, spars, spwawn, specks, spelled, splay, spore, stacks, stalled, staple, stink, stone, stood, sucks, suns, surface, tadpole, tainted, taupo, taxis, teeming, telecine, telecom, tending, tested, thanks, thumbed, tones, tort, totem, trading, treated, treks, tribes, trot, truck, tubing, tulane, tulsa, turn, undone, undyed, union, united, urchin, vandals, vanish, variance, viborg, voices, wagtail, waxy, weaning, wichita, winder, wolds, wreckage, yeoman

Value 74
ablation, abominable, accesses, according, accretes, accursed, acquire, additive, adequate, adverse, advocacy, aerobatic, agonised, aileron, ailment, allergen, alleys, alloyed, angular, antedated, antennae, anyone, archival, artefact, assayed, attained, audibly, audits, aurora, avoidance, aztecs, bagpiper, ballerina, balmoral, bardsey, basalts, bathtub, beauty, beginner, belongs, benchers, between, biannual, billund, bitter, bombers, bosnian, bottle, boules, braggart, breakup, breton, bruise, brutal, burns, bushes, camphor, canners, canopy, caprices, cartload, carving, causing, censor, centered, chariot, chesapeake, chests, chilling, chloride, chordate,

clarify, clinician, clocking, cloning, clonmel, closet, clouds, cocktail, collages, conceding, concur, condoned, connect, cooking, cordite, coups, coveted, cratered, craving, crested, crisped, cross, cubist, cuddling, curbing, cwmbran, dandruff, deepest, deflect, delighted, demarcated, devalued, diagnose, dialogue, diction, diffused, discharge, diverged, donkey, doodles, dragoon, drastic, dressed, drills, drown, ductile, dushanbe, dutiable, eighty, element, elevated, enchanted, energy, english, engulfed, enteric, erratic, error, escaping, ethereal, etudes, eurasia, exclude, exiles, falconer, families, fastened, fictive, fifties, finished, flamelike, flanking, flapper, florin, flukes, follicle, foreign, fruit, fujairah, fuller, fusible, gatwick, girdles, glaciers, gliders, glitz, globule, godson, goitre, gorilla, gospel, granite, greater, greets, greys, haricot, harlot, hawarden, heavens, heroine, hexagon, hiccough, hokkaido, holiday, hoopoe, horns,

hundred, hurrah, idyllic, ilkley, illicit, impish, implacable, increase, indecent, infuse, inhaling, initial, jailers, jerking, jesus, jewels, jewish, jolly, jotted, jury, killing, labelling, lacewing, landmark, largish, lasers, legally, legatees, lenses, lesion, licorice, likely, linnet, loaves, london, looms, lounge, lymph, macaroni, maghull, mandarin, mangoes, manifold, mannered, marital, martial, masking, masonic, mastiff, measles, melanoma, melody, menorah, merino, merited, messiah, moulded, moves, mutt, nebulas, nicknamed, notable, nuclear, nugget, nuts, obedient, objects, oblates, occult, okinawa, oleander, operas, opium, ordnance, oregon, organs, oriole, pairing, pallor, parables, parcels, parent, parts, payload, peering, pendant, penny, photo, pianos, pinnacle, pitted, pledging, point, polkas, pollen, polls, pommel, poses, pounce, preacher, prize, proud, pulped, pupil, quota, raiders, ranching, ranking, rapper, rattan, readily, refuse, relent, reliefs, renewed, repeated, retaken, retold, rout, rubies, ruler, sabotaged, sailor, salmon, sarcasm, savages, scanner, seaway, semblance, shaggier, shaping, shearer, sheffield, shines, shingle, shirt, shoals, showed, signet, simple, sizable, skater, slimmed, sliding, sloth, snails, snatched, sneeze, soils, songs, sparked, speedy, spent, sprat, spur, squeak, stabbing, stayed, steady, steeped, strap, streak, stuck, stun, suite, surged, swarm, talking, tamils, tangier, tantra, tarot, tearing, tenant, terraced, testee, theism, thicker, threw, tinges, toucan, tour, traps, trauma, trawl, trekked, trevi, turbid, unafraid, unbelief, unchecked, unclear, uncles, unpick, upkeep, upside, uptake, usual, varduz, varies, vassal, videos, wandered, warms, weapon, weaver, weirs, welding, whaling, widens, widnes, widow, winkle, wires, wombat, yields, zairean

Value 77
abrasive, absorbable, abundant, acceleerated, account, accusing, addictive, admirals, adults, affective, airborn, aircrash, alphabetic, alsatian,

analyse, anguilla, annealing, appliance, applicable, aquifer, arachnids, ardour, arguing, arising, armpit, arraigned, arrived, asphalt, atlases, attaches, aubretia, barrelled, barrow, baskets, beatings, belgravia, besieging, betting, binaries, birkenhead, bivalved, blarney, bluebuck, booty, borers, botanical, botany, bothered, boulder, bouts, brasov, brazing, breadths, briefly, broadly, broadside, broccoli, brushed, buffers, bundles, butcher, calendars, canaveral, capsule, carcinoma, catacombs, catchers, catering, catkins, chamaeleon, chambermaid, chancery, changeful, character, chemist, cherry, chervil, chillies, chimney, chiselled, christ, ciliary, cinematic, cleaners, cleanser, cloths, clydebank, coasts, coblenz, cockpit, cockroach, compete, compiled, conclude, condemned, cookies, council, court, creating, creeping, creoles, crisis, cromlech, crouched, cyclone, daytime, dealmaking, deciphered, declining, deferent, delaying, designs, detectable, diaphragm, disabling, disciple, disuse, divers, dopamine, dozier, drives, drying, earthy, ecliptic, economic, efficient, elicits, elixir, emeralds, emporia, emulate, enclosed, endangered, engineer, equalled, erectile, esplanade, evokes, excuse, exeter, exhibit, exist, exits, expended, expire, facsimile, failings, fascist, fatally, fathers, feelings, felony, felspar, fiefdoms, financing, firebrand, fisheye, flamingo, flexing, flogging, foraging, forbidden, fought, fresno, friary, funeral, gamblers, gamecocks, gasohol, gastric, germans, girobank, glory, gokstad, graduate, greaves, groomed, group, grown, guadalajara, guadalcanal, gullet, gutted, hammers, harlow, harrier, harsher, hazards, headlines, hearsay, herders, hertzhovered, hoylake, humps, icebreaker, identical, idiolect, imagines, imitate, impart, impeding, impinged, impose, inaudible, injure, issued, jarring, javanese, jester, jetfoil, jointed, judaism, keflavik, kerry, kimono, kneeling, known, lacquer, landward, lanolin, latest, lenders, leukemia, levelled, lifting, liners, literal, llanelli, loops, lutes, mammalian, mandates, mannheim, marketed, matter, meanest, meditate, menagerie, migrated, moccasin, moldavia, moslem, mouth, mucus, muscled, muses, narrate, narwhal, neatly, negating, nematode, nepalese, nests, nigerian, nights, nijmegen, nuances, nurse, obeying, obstacle, oddity, offally, orbital, ostend, ounces, ouzo, pagemaker, pancreas, parabolic, parakeet, parallel, parapet, pardoned, parley, partial, pauper, peacetime, peanut, pearly, permeable, perugia, phones, pillared, pimlico, player, polite, pools, power, prelate, press, print, probate, quart, quasar, rackets, radiates, rafflesia, railheads, raising, reacting, readings, realism, regency, repelled, replay, research, revered, roaming, robins, rocking, rooted, rosy, runes, sackbut, sacrufuced, salty, schedule, sciences, scopes, scrambled, seabirds, seagoing, seagull, seaspeak, seismic, sewing, shipped, shoeing, shoot, shops, shrewd, shuffle, siberian, sicily, sideline, silly, skirt, slender, sloop, smacking, smiles, solved, spends, spicing, spilled, spins, spool, sprain, stabler, staging, stamina, stands, stars, stocked, stoned, store, stow, strife, studded, sucker, sunni, surfaced, swaffham, swayed, swift, synod, talkies, tampico, taoism, taught, teapot, temper, theater, theatre, thereof, thermal, things, thoracic, tianjin, tinker, tiring, trent, trochaic, troll, tsars, unbalanced, unchanged, unesco, unseeded, ussr, uvula, vacancies, valley, vibrate, vowel, vying, walking, wants, weakly, wearing, wetted, whoop, widgeon, wobbler, wound, wraps, wretch, wrong, xinhua, xining, yarns, yeomen, zodiacs

Value 78
abdication, aberavon, ability, brupt, absinthe, accepting, accessible, accidents, achieving, acquired, adaptive, adjudicate, adrenalin, adviser, aggrieved, alaskans, alcoholic, aldeburgh, almonds, almoner, amalgamated, ambrosia, amuses, anchors, androgen, animism, annelids, annoyed, anodyne, apennine, applies, approach, archery, artful, assent, assigned, assume, athletic, averages, backroom, beforehand, belarus, believer, belmopan, bermudan, berserk, bicycles, biomass, biplanes, blindfold, blitzed, bolton, boyish, bracknell, breathes, breslau, brewing, briton, broadens, bruised, budgets, building, burbot, burner, burrs, butler, buying, calculate, capacity, caption, carrion, cartels, caskets, ceilings, channelled, charlatan, chassis, cheerful, cheques, chester, childhood, ciphers, civets, clapping, clarets, classes, cleveland, coldest,

colicky, colleges, collider, column, commando, comrades, conceited, concert, confidence, confirm, connacht, crackers, crafting, credits, criccieth, crows, crucified, crumbled, crushed, cuckolded, culling, cusps, dandelion, darkest, dazzled, deceiving, decision, delegates, demagogue, denying, depending, deport, derivable, despite, diagnosed, differing, dimples, directs, discharged, ditty, divert, dividing, dolphin, dominance, dorking, doubles, dragons, dreamlike, dressage, dropped, duties, easiest, educates, effector, elector, ellipse, embryo, emerging, emigrate, endless, enjoyed, epicycle, etchers, evacuate, excluded, exudes, fairest, fascinate, fewest, fielders, fingers, fitter, flagship, flagstaff, fleeting, florence, fluent, follies, forts, fretted, fringes, frost, fungicide, furies, galaxies, gamebirds, garment, gathers, giessen, genomes, goblins, goldfinch, gowns, gradient, greenock, gross, grumble, gujarat, hardware, hedgehogs, heralding, hillside, hindlegs, hoddesden, holyhead, homely, hopper, hugely, hurls, imagery, imagist, immense, immobile, impune, incident, inciter, incomes, increased, infidels, infected, infused, insider, integer, ionize, irascible, islands, joining, jokers, keratin, kingly, knighted, krakatoa, laboured, lefkosia, legalism, lemons, lesser, leukaemia, liberals, linkages, little, locarno, lofty, longing, lucerne, magdeburg, managers, mapmaker, mariner, marrakech, mature, megabyte, melons, merely, miners, misnamed, mistake, molars, musical, mutes,

myelin, mythic, negros, nimbus, nominal, obviated, october, onyx, otter, overhead, paranoiac, paranoid, passer, peacemaker, peafowl, peewit, pencils, pendent, pidgins, pithy, plump, podium, ponies, poplar, precedence, prefix, prized, pruned, publican, purer, quote, railroad, razor, recessed, redating, reflected, refused,
reindeer, remedies, remove, renewal, repent, repose, revise, rewarded, rifleman, ringing, rooks, rouse, rover, rust, ruts, salute, sandbars, scallop, scarlet, schist, scorer, scorned, scout, screams, searches, seceders, secrecy, selfish, selling, semitic, severed, sexing, shackles, shaolin, shires, sickles, silicate, siting, sizes, slaves, slouch, slowed, slugs, smelted, sobers, solemn, solids, spangled, spares, sparse, spatial, spears, spry, squat, stables, stamped, start, stockade, suicidal, suited, tampere, tasmania, tents, thefts, thirds, tigers, tolls, tomsk, tooth, tory, travel, tredegar, tudor, tulip, tundra, tuscan, twigs, ulcers, umbrian, unseen, untamed, uphill, vaccinate, validated, vendor, verified, views, vintage, violas, visible, waiver, waltham, warmer, wasps, weakens, whelks, widely, wieldy, wiping, wives, wobbles, yiddish

Value 80
aardwolf, aborigine, absolved, absorber, accomplice, adirondack, affording, afrikaans, aground, airship, allergy, alluding, allying, almost, amazonia, anglicans, answer, anthems,

appearance, applauded, ardennes, aromatic, arrears, assembled, atlantic, augsberg, avocados, backgammon, banquet, baptism, barricades, bastille, bastion, bedevilled, behavior, belladonna, benefits, benidorm, betrayed, bilateral, biochemical, bloomer, blurred, bobolink, boilers, boosted, borehole, bossy, bourse, brainchild, bringing, bronze, brooks, buddhism, bumbling, burst, bushbaby, butyl, camcorder, camembert, cancelling, candidates, cannery, cannons, carnival, casement, casinos, catheter, catmint, cavity, cellist, changeling, charting, chihuahua, clauses, clemency, clevedon, cloudy, coercive, collars, combines, compacted, conceived, conduct, confers, conflated, congenial, conwy, coolant, corset, coypu, crawler, creator, cretans, crowbar, cuisine, cupboard, cutbacks, cyanides, daredevil, deaneries, defenders, deserted, destined, diarist, diligent, dipoles, disbarred, dismayed, dispatch, divorced, divulge, dredgers, dulwich, eardrum, earners, eccentric, ecstatic, elegancies, elucidate, embarking, eminent, endows, entails, entrance, episodic, erupt, escort, europe, excrete, exhumed, exiling, fainting, falklands, falsely, farmers, featured, feckless, ferries, fighting, filament, flints, fossil, fractals, funny, gallery, gallons, gannets, geodesy, girders, glanders, gloves, goldfish, grasps, greenland, grunt, guessed, guises, gunboat, gunfire, gymkhana, habitats, hapless, hardening, heartbeat, heathens, helpful, heresy, heritable, heswall, hitter, hoisted, hornet, horny, hotly, hygienic, inducted, inhibited, inhuman, injects, inlays, input, inroads, insipid, invading, invalided, invoked, jetty, juggler, karting, kennels, kidnapped, kindling, knives, landings, landlord, landslide, laptop, largely, latency, layers, leaflets, learning, letter, lifelong, limerick, limoges, llangefni, locally, lockerbie, lunatic, lyrical, magnates, mainframe, majestic, manors, marburg, marmot, meadows, meantime, mellow, melting, mendips, messina, metabolic, meters, metres, minaret, miracles, modifies, moment, moors, mosul, moving, mudlark, myself, neckwear, noblemen, nutmeg, nylon, oboist, obtains, offending, offering, officials, opening, operate, ottawa, ovarian, overt, paganism, palermo, party, patios, patois, pedagogical, peelers, perching, pious, pitches, planner, plastic, plural, policy, posing, potted, preloaded, presided, primes, proved, psalms, pulls, quaking, racetrack, ransom, reactor, realized, reappear, rebirth, reclaims, rectum, refracted, rejects, rejoined, relapsed, relates, relays, relieved, replaceable, resaleable, revenged, revoked, rippled, rockies, roller, romans, rooms, salient, salons, sanders, savannah, scents, scilly, seafaring, sector, senior, serfdom, setbacks, shaving, sheaths, shining, short, sixth, slayer, sleeper, sleight, slovak, smaller, smells, solos, sower, speeches, spiky, spoken, stealer, steels, stilt, strabane, subject, sundial, swagger, swelled, swore, tactician, talavera, targeted, tartu, tavern, tbilisi, telford, tentacle, thesis, throne, tilts, tonics, tragedy, trances, trapped, trends, tricks, triple, tusked, undecidable, unseat, upbraided, ushered, values, veering, vents, viaduct, vicenza, voter, walsall, warbles, weather, welcomed, widest, wildlife, wimps, winding, wiring, worse, yankees

Value 81
abandoning, abducting, acolyte, actions, activate, aerofoil, allaying, always, amarillo, amphibole, analysed, angelfish, annular, anomaly, another, appealing, agreement, arrest, arrival, ascents, audiences, augment, avoiding, awesome, awkward, axioms, beginning, bergamot, betony, biathlon, bizerta, blackbirds, bombings, borders, brazos, breezy, busts, calcutta, capitals, cardinals, carotene, carriages, caryatid, castille, castlebar, catechism, census, centipede, cerebellar, cervix, chicory, chorales, choughs, clansmen, clasping, climbers, coaster, coincides, colleague, colonial, competed, concerned, concluded, confess, confiding, cortical, coulomb, course, cousin, cowardice, critics, croatian, crooks, crust, damascus, defection, defoliated, deliberate, denounce, designer, desolate, despised, detailing, dictates, discerned, diseases, disused, divorcee, dockyard, dollars, dominate, dorset, doubts, downy, duckling, effective, ejection, elderly, elective, elephant, emulated, engendered, enigmatic, enlarges, enters, enticing, envoy, evacuees, evolve, exalts, excavate, excitable,

excused, exerted, expels, expired, explain, explode, extended, eyeballs, factional, fairbanks, fashioned, fatalism, feasting, feldspar, ferrite, fillers, firefly, flagellate, flapping, flatfish, flights, forgot, galleys, generals, geochemical, germicidal, glimpse, godless, govern, graduated, graphics, grenadier, guarding, guatemala, halogens, handbills, handicapped, harbors, harmonic, haywain, hearings, heretical, hermetic, highway, holders, honest, hooligan, hooter, hosts, hounds, hours, howler, hudson, hydrate, idylls, imitated, immoral, impacts, imposed, incredible, indolence, inducing, inferno, ingrained, injured, inmates, interface, ironical, irony, isolate, jewess, jewry, jiangsu, keswick, keyboard, keyhole, kinsman, kirkuk, landlocked, lavender, lawrence, leanings, leasehold, legalized, legions, lerwick, levers, ligament, limasol, litany, locating, lowland, lumps, maintain, malaysia, manuals, marauder, margins, masons, mastoid, matron, medially, medicines, mescaline, metrical, minty, moderate, moneyed, moselle, motor, moult, mourn, mowing, mullard, myopic, narrated, nautical, newts, noises, novella, nursed, nyborg, oarsman, oblique, obtainable, officers, ongoing, opting, orient, orissa, orphaned, ovary, panting, papist, paraclete, parsecs, pauses, pedagogue, penchant, percent, permit, phuket, physics, pickers, pickling, piercing, piloted, pintail, placings, plagues, plasmas, plums, poetical, powder, preaching, preceding, predicate, prelude, probing, problem, profile, proms, queens, racially, raincoat, randstad, rapping, rarest, reasoned, recalling, redesign, reducing, refuges, regional, renaming, replete, rescinded, resent, residue, resigned, rests, resume, revels, revive, ridicule, rights, riots, ritual, rivals, rocketed, rounded, ruins, ruling, sadness, sandfly, sandwich, scanning, scheduled, schematic, scratched, seafowl, seaweeds, seawise, senses, service, settle, shadings, shakers, sharps, shearing, shifts, shots, shovel, shuffled, shuns, signals, silicon, similar, sinus, sinful, siphon, siskin, skting, slipped, slump, sodium, sorted, source, soybean, spender, spokane, square, squaw, stances, standard, stanza, steamer, steppe, sticks, stool, stored, stove, strain, straw, strode, stucco, stuffed, style, sublime, superb, surer, swahili, tabernacle, talented, talons, tangent, telegram, tennis, theist, thinks, thrift, tithes, toboggan, toilet, tools, torbay, toward, tower, tracts, trains, trios, tropic, tubule, typeface, ugandans, unbearable, unblended, uneven, upset, vacuum, valetta, valves, verdict, votes, vulgar, warts, washing, watchdog, wattle, weaving, weekly, weighted, whipped, wirral, wizard, wrote, yardbird, zimbabwe

Value 83
acerbity, adaptogen, adjoining, adrenaline, aeration, aerospace, aesthete, affirming, agility, airfields, airless, aldehydes, alderfly, aleutian, allegedly, amassing, ambition, americans, analogies, annulled, apathetic, aprons, arbroath,

aroused, arranges, asexual, aspects, assets, assure, attaching, attends, attract, auction, author, autism, bachelors, banbury, bandicoot, banishing, baptized, barbarism, bayous, beatlemania, belvoir, beneficent, benelux, berkeley, bermudas, berthing, biscuit, blazers, boxers, brasses, bravura, breakfast, broadcast, bulkheads, burdens, burmese, campaigns, capsized, captains, carbonated, caution, censored, chateaux, churns, cinnamon, circuit, clamour, clearest, clerihew, cockatoo, collapse, colonnade, colorado, comedians, comment, concealing, concrete, condensed, condoms, confuse, connected, console, convex, covert, cowboy, coyote, creative, crippled, criteria, crossed, curitiba, curer, dampening, dartboard, debtors, decathlete, deficiency, dependant, deprived, detaining, diaspora, digests, dimmest, discreet, discrete, docklands, dozens, dragooned, dreamers, driving, drowned, elaborated, election, elision, elongated, emblematic, embroiled, entente, ephemeral, epidemics, epithet, epitome, estonia, ethiopia, eugenics, evasive, evenly, evoking, exacting, execute, expands, expelled, fairway, faithful, favour, fiercely, fifieth, firmly, flageolet, flouted, fluidics, flutes, follow, football, forest, foster, founder, franchise, freeborn, freeway, freezer, fruited, gangplank, gaslight, gently, geomancy, germany, geysir, glassy, guangxi, hanover, haphazard, harbour, hardship, harrow, haunts, heartland, heiress, helpers, homesick, hurried, hydrangea, ideograph, idiomatic, ignites, immured, imperial, implies, inactive, infants, ingested, inhabitable, inherit, inscribed, invited, iridium, isobars, jealous, jubilees, jumper, knitted, knowable, koreans, lagoons, landmass, launches, laureate, legation, lessened, lilting, litres, ljubljana, lonely, looking, magnifies, magnons, mailmerge, mammoth, manorial, mansfield, marries, marshes, massacred, medalist, medleys, memphis, mendicant, methyl, monkey, motto, mount, movies, mullet, narcotic, navigated, needless, negative, negroes, nerves, neuter, nexus, nouns, obscure, occupy, orally, orbits, ordinance, pacifist, pageants, painter, pansies, panthers, paradise, paramedical, parochial, parsees, parson, pastime, pelvis, perceive, perhaps, phalanges, phonemic, phoney, pickets, plying, pointed, pompeii, postage, postal, potomac, poundage, poundal, practical, prayer, precept, prepared, preset, prevail, psychic, puckered, pyres, quays, raccoon, radiating, radishes, rampant, rashly, reactive, recluse, referenced, referral, refound, regarding, reigning, relocated, renders, replicas, resembled, reusable, revocable, rivalled, riveted, rotated, routed, sandpit, sardonic, satyr, screens, seacoast, segment, seizes, selects, serials, severn, sewerage, shepherd, shetland, shout, shrimp, signalled, sinking, smiling, smoky, soaring, softer, south, specify, spells, spinet, spiny, spits, splendid, spring, squalid, stalinabad, stalls, stampede, stiffer, stork, stray, streaked, studs, subsided, suburb, suffrage, swarmed, swept, swims, syllabic, tactful, tallow, tapping, tawny, tayside, tearful, tempted, tenets, tenure, terpene, tests, texans, theorbo, thereby, thumbs, toured, tracking, trays, treats, tunis, twitch, unaware, unbeatable, unifies, units, unripe, upward, vagrant, vainly, vector, vehicles, violet, visor, wagoner, waiting, warlock, warmth, watchman, watts, waukegan, waxbill, wharfedale, wheeling, widowed, widths, wielding, wilful, winner, wisdom, wishes, within, wooing, wrapped, wrecker, ypres

Value 84
abstract, abundances, accompanied, adjusted, airflow, alderney, alkaloids, alloys, alphabets, alphorn, amniotic, amount, amusing, analyze, androids, anteater, arizona, arkansas, arterial, assays, assemblage, attains, audacity, averaging, awaiting, azores, backwater, banality, baritone, basically, bastards, batchelor, beastly, benzyl, betrayal, beverages, bitumen, blackburn, blankets, blasting, bloodshed, blotches, bolivian, bombastic, bosons, boyhood, breasts, breathing, brindisi, broadest, brooding, calamity, camberley, cameroon, camouflage, canvases, capture, catatonia, ceullular, centers, centres, charity, chengzu, chingford, chlorine, chooses, clambering, cleansing, clumps, cocoons, cognates, coincidence, colombian, colony, colour, combating, commune, comply, conciliar, conform, consul, contended, convey, cosmos, coughing, cranefly, craters, crevices, crocodile,

curling, curtail, cyclonic, darlings, daughter, dedication, degenerate, deletion, delights, delivered, densely, descending, describes, designate, detonate, devonian, diachronic, didjeridu, dilation, disgorge, disparaged, distended, donating, doubling, dovecot, downbeat, dummies, dumping, dutchman, educating, elstree, elucidated, emanating, embassy, endogamy, endored, engulfs, ephedrine, excreted, expandable, expanse, expose, extant, exuding, farmhands, fatness, feisty, fervor, figurehead, fishers, flimsy, floating, foolish, footman, forays, forty, fouling, fragment, freezes, freshman, fringing, frozen, fusion, garnets, gascony, gazette, geophagy, gestalt, gimmicks, gipsies, glasgow, godfather, goshawk, gourds, granary, graphite, grievance, grimly, hamster, handicraft, harness, hatchets, heathers, himalayan, hobgoblin, hogmanay, hokusai, holborn, hooves, horses, husky, idolized, ilfracombe, incoming, indicates, ineligible, informed, invent, islets, jazzband, jesuit, kagoshima, kernels, knocking, laments, lantern, lawyer, lecture, leipzig, leningrad, lessees, lesson, librarian, librium, lightened, linings, litter, looser, madrigals, mahogany, mammary, manners, marshy, maternal, matting, mechanize, medically, mediums, meissen, memorable, merits, methods, michaelmas, microbes, midnight, million, miserable, misses, mister, mitigate, mitres, modeller, modular, motels, motive, moulds, navvy, nemesis, niceties, noodles, notches, numeral, olduvai, operated, orifices, orleans, ousted, pandemics, parsing, particle, patagonia, patron, pekinese, pennant, penzance, perfume, perished, pheasant, phonics, pigment, pilgrim, pinafore, pincers, playing, polyp, precipice, preclude, predicted, premier, princes, profit, props, qualified, quicker, ramsgate, rasping, readout, realist, rebelling, recombine, reconcile, recurs, redness, redwood, reformed, regaining, releases, reliably, repeats, replies, reproach, resins, rhomboid, richmond, rigidly, roofing, rosebud, salaries, salerno, salesman, sampler, savers, scenario, seafoods, searching, selectable, semantic, sermon, sevens, seville, shores, shows, sifting, sirens, sizing, slaving, slighted, slums, sniffing, societal, sparks, specials, specimen, spectacle, splashed, spoilage, states, stays, strange, submit, sucking, suffered, sunday, sunken, swung, tilored, tangshan, tastes, tensile, theorem, throw, tibesti, timely, toasted, tokens, tomato, topple, tracers, treatable, trigger, tripled, troop, trunk, umbrella, undergo, undoing, unharmed, unused, uplift, useful, utter, vampire, venerable, verdun, vietnam, violate, visual, wallabies, wanders, wardens, weakest, whites, wools, worth, zimmer

Value 86

abilities, accounted, actuarial, adolescence, adopting, aggravated, airliner, algerians, allowance, alongside, altering, alveolar, amygdalin, anabolism, anarchism, anecdotes, anemones, anglicize, anthrax, antiwar, aridity, armour, aspirin, astute, attacking, avalanches, aviator, barbitone, barograph, batallion, beefeaters, beguiling, belatedly, billiards, bimetallic, biopsy, blackness, bodyline, bohemians, borough, bounding, brittle, brother, brownie, bumblebees, bungling, butchered, butter, calmness, canoeist, capacities, capacitor, capybaras, cartoon, carvers, cashless, cataracts, catatonic, celestial, centigrade, chairlift, challenges, chequered, cherwell, chicanery, chorley, citizen, clipping, cliques, clowns, clydeside, coalfields, combining, commander, commends, comparable, compass, compose, concubine, conduit, confidant, connived, convict, cookers, coppices, cornfield, cornices, cornish, corpora, cortona, corunna, cucumber, curtain, custard, cysts, dartford, daylight, deadweight, debility, deflation, defoliant, densest, depletes, deployed, diffracts, disclose, display, dissuaded, ditties, drinking, duluth, duress, dwelling, ecumenical, eightfold, emphases, empirical, employ, energetic, enforceable, engineered, enmity, ensured, envisaged, epidural, epistle, evidences, exchanges, exhibited, existed, facilitate, fantasy, festive, finalized, flotsam, flowing, fluency, foetus, footing, forceful, formula, fowling, fraction, freiburg, frenchmen, frontage, frontal, fuelling, fujiyama, fukuoka, fungicidal, geological, geology, globally, grasmere, gravelled, grooved, grouped, groves, grower, guildhall, hainault, haslemere, healthier, herdsmen, hermitage, highlander, horrific, hotter, humbling, hunter, hurdler, hussar, ignorance, immersed, inanimate, indexing, infinite, infixes, inflates, influx, infringed, inkwell, innings, insight, integral, intense, ironing, jordanian, killers, kilogram, kinship, kyoto, lacquered, legorno, leitrim, lettuce, licenses, lighting, lisping, loathing, lobbying, lordly, lyrics, maligning, margarine, marihuana, marlins, massifs, mastix, measured, memorial, messing, minting, mismanaged, mismatch, missile, misty, misuse, mnemonic, molecule, mongolia, mortgage, motion, mounds, mouthed, mullahs, national, newest, nineteen, noctuid, noticeable, nuisance, observe, occidental, oeuvre, omitted, onions, oppose, optimal, orchards, ordinate, organics, ossified, overlaid, paediatric, palisades, paralleled, paraplegia, pedagogics, pediment, penguin, periods, petrol, petty, petunia, phrases, pipeline, pirhanas, pitching, planter, plumes, polemical, pondweed, pontiff, poodles, popper, powered, poznan, pressed, pretence, priming, printed, produced, propfan, prudence, psycho, punches, purges, pygmy, query, racketeer, radiator, radiogram, ranchers, rapiers, ravioli, receives, recorder, recover, rectify, redoubled, reflux, refugees, relating, remarkable, reminder, removal, repairs, republic, researched, respect, retains, romany, rotor, rowing, santiago, saxifraga, scarcely, scatter, sceptre, sculls, seasonal, shocking, shopman, sibyls, silences, silicone, similes, singly, sinning, skirted, slopes, snakebite, soluble, someone, sooner, souls, spanish, spearheaded, spectre, spires, spreader, stainer, stairs, stalker, statue, staunch, staves, steely, steers, stews, stowed, subset, sweetie, symbol, tabulated, tanzania, teachings, technician, teesside, tempered, tenths, thorax, threading, thrived, thyme, timers, timbres, tokyo, tories, triangle, tricky, trilby, tufts, tunics, tunnel, typical, unforced, unmanned, upheaval, uppsala, valuing, velvet, venues, vibrant, voodoo, wapping, wardrobe, warning, waster, waters, wayside, weekends, welders, whalers, whinchat, willing, wisps, wizened, woodlice, works, wounded, wretched, xerox, yearly, yukon, zither

Value 88

aboriginal, absconding, accession, accretion, acrostic, advisor, affiliates, agitating, agnostic, agreement, allegiances, allergies, ambushes, analyzed, anchovy, anglesey, anguished, animating, annexing, antelope, antenatal, antennas, antidote, apostle, appalling, appendages, appreciable, archangels, artificial, assigns, auditor, aviemore, ballroom, baptists, bellows, bequeathed, bestrode, birdsong, bisecting, bishops, bittern, blameless, bombshell, bonfires, brittania, brokers, budapest, bulwark, busily, california, camouflaged, capacious, captured, carcasses, caregiver, castilian, caucasus, cauldron, cavities, ceaseless, cedarwood, celsius, championed, chopping, cigarette, cirrus, clarify, clearings, clothing, coalescing, coatings, coherent, cohesion, collagens, complex, condors, conference, conferred, copenhagen, coroner, crediton, crickets, crooner, crudely, curves, defamation, degenerated, denoting, deposit, deptford, deriving, designated, designing, detonated, developed, dielectric, dignity, disagreeable, discarding, displaces, dissected, divining, doctoral, doctrine, dolerite, domestic, donetsk, dramatics, dreamtime, dresser, dugout, dunkirk, dwarfish, dynamics, ebullience, eclipses, edinburgh, electrical, eliciting, eliminate, embolism, empathy, enchanter, enjoys, enlisted, enzyme, equates, essays, eurasian, exacerbated, excellence, exercise, exodus, expendable, expense, expert, exposed, extent, factory, faculty, fastener, feathery, federally, feminism, fillings, fixings, fizzled, flashgun, flowered, focuses, folksy, forbidding, forebrain, forfeited, formalin, fourth, fretful, friezes, fungus, furry, galleries, gamester, gazetted, gelignite, geometer, geranium, ghosts, gibraltar, girlhood, glamorgan, gleanings, globular, glyceride, gophers, grandest, grandeur, grasses, greatly, greenbelt, grounded, guadelupe, hammering, hardness, hardwood, heresies, highlight, hindering, hoddesdon, holdings, holiest, hoodlum, hormone, hostile, howling, husbands, hyacinth, inflammable, informal, inshore, interim, invert, inwards, jetties, jockeys, jungles, kissing, knights, labours, lacework, lameness, laurels, lectured, lemurs, liquefied, listened, loadbearing, longbow, looping, lorry, losers, luzon, maidenhood, manchuria, marauding, marijuana, maritime, marketable, marrow, maryland, massive, matrices, mechanized, messages, meteoric, mexicans, mimicking, minidisk, minnow, minors, mitigated, mixers, moorhen, mormon, moscow, murdered, murky, muslin, mutual, nameless, nesting, neuralgia, nomadism, notables, nowhere, objectified, objector, obsessed, occasioned, octagonal, oilseeds, orkney, pamplona, pangolin, paradigms, parrot, parties, peoples, perfumed, persona, photon, pianist, piglets, pirates, pleasant, ploughed, plover, podgorica, poison, policeman, policies, polished, pooling, poppy, ports, posited, potsdam, pragmatic, precinct, preening, program, prolific, proper, purified, purple, pushes, putrid, pyrex, queues, quipped, raccoons, ramblers, raptor, ratings, ravines, rearward, rebounded, receptacle, recombined, reconciled, redress, reflects, refreshed, regents, remembered, repartee, repeater, restate, retailer, revalued, revert, rewards, rhymes, rigour, romances, salamander, salesmen, sanity, scatty, sceptical, scotland, scourge, seascapes, seedless, semifinal, semolina, serves, shamrock, sharers, shower, sikhism, skimmer, slows, sluices, smiths, smokey, smoking, smuggled, softened, solely, songbird, spectacled, spending, sport, sprayed, spurn, stamps, standing, staring, steaming, steeper, sterile, stiffened, stigmas, stings, stitched, stoker, stroke, studio, suchlike, sudanese, suits, sulky, swoop, syllable, tankards, tankers, tempos, tennis, terrific, texts, thickly, thieves, thinly, thinner, thither, tidying, tintagel, toppled, torches, torun, towing, tragedies, tripped, truffle, trump, tsetse, uncaused, underdog, underlie, unending, unites, unpaired, unready, vanguard, venoms, verruca, verses, violated, vision, visited, vitamin, vitebsk, volts, volume, vomited, wanderer, wanting, warders, warwick, whores, wigton, window, woodland, worms, wreaking, xinjiang, yeovil, zooms

Value 89
abbreviated, abduction, abhorrence, academically, accusers, acronym, actuary, additional, alexandria, alimony, allegheny, allotted, alloway, amendment, amongst, amplifier, anatomical, anatomy, anchoring, anomalies, answered, antarctic, antedates, anthracene, antigens, antlers, anyway, appendix, argentina, arranging, ascendancy, assignable, audiogram, august, austere, austria, bassist, beaumaris, benefactor, bequest, biogenetic, bluetit, briefings, broadway, buckingham, burundi, calumny, carcinogen, caresses, castigated, catalogued, cattleman, censured, chauffeur, cheltenham, chilblains, churchman, coastland, collects, collegiate, combatant, complete, conducted, conifers, conjoined, converge, convinced, copying, counsel, courier, crayfish, creepers, crimping, crowing, crusader, cupbearer, cushion, deceptive, defensive, defrauding, deposing, descendant, descents,

despoiled, dethrone, devising, devolved, diffuses, directing, disappear, disembodied, dispatched, diuretic, diverges, dolgellau, dossier, dresses, dusty, earliest, earthly, effluent, efforts, elevates, emotive, encourage, ensuing, entitled, erection, erupted, escorted, essences, estates, esthetic, examiner, explicable, fatherland, felicity, fictional, filters, fingering, finishes, firearms, fireflies, fluting, flybys, foragers, forensic, forever, forsaken, gallows, gathering, gentry, geographic, gradation, grassy, greenfinch, handbooks, harfleur, heartbreak, heaviest, himalayas, hologram, hurling, igniting, incubus, influence, insects, invest, ivory, jawless, joyful, kitchens, knotted, launching, leisure, lizards, location, loosened, losses, loudly, lovably, magnificence, markedly, mellowed, memory, microfiche, millennia, misery, modules, months, mottled, musician, musket, musky, mussel, mutant, mystic, narrow, nectarine, neuchatel, nicaraguan, nicknames, nicotine, nightfall, notably, opacity, operant, option, oracular, orinoco, ovaries, overlap, oversee, parasite, parity, pastor, pellets, persuade, phallus, phenols, phosgene, placement, pockets, populace, portable, posts, potion, pounds, pours, premiere, premised, prongs, proofs, provide, quinine, radicalism, railway, rainwear, raisins, ransomed, reagents, reappeared, rebuses, reckoner, redaction, redshift, regulate, religion, renown, rentals, replicate, reputed, rescuer, residual, retraces, revival, ribaldry, ripping, robots, romford, sandflies, sardines, sardinian, scarring, scenery, scramjet, screaming, secrets, sediment, seizing, sentenced, sequence, seraphim, sergeant, sewers, sexism, shadows, shrugged, signboard, signify, sketcher, snapper, snout, sonatas, spartan, spots, sprawl, squire, stafford, starved, stilted, stokes, stops, strict, study, stump, stupid, subjected, success, suicides, suitable, summer, supple, surges, swiss, sworn, tallest, tectonic, terraces, terrible, thickens, tilburg, tonsil, totalled, trampled, treaty, tremor, treves, tribune, trifles, trough, turbine, turks, tuxedo, twinned, ulcerated, unbridled, underhand, unity, unleashed, unmatched, untaxed, valour, variables, verifiable, viewing,vipers, virginia, virus, visceral, voluble, vyborg, walkers, wartime, weakening, weathered, wellbeing, winter, wishing, withheld, woodcock, wrist, writs, yeasts, yokohama, youth, yunnan

Value 90
acetylene, acrylics, admittance, advocates, aesthetic, affinity, alchemist, alluvial, alphabetical, altarpiece, amnestied, analgesics, anglicized, antarctica, antibody, antihero, antitank, approx, appulse, archdiocese, armory, arrested, artichoke, artifices, ascertain, athletes, augmented, aurally, autumn, balloons, barriers, benedictine, bicarbonate, bioethics, boldness, boomerang, bordeaux, brethren, brewers, brisling, brochure, bromley, builders, bunkers, burgers, buyers, catechetical, catfishes, catholics, catterick, ceasefires, celebrates, cementing,

chandlery, chapters, cheapness, checklist, choosing, chromatic, citrus, clappers, clumpy, coalminer, combative, comfort, commences, commute, compares, composed, confessed, confident, conscience, consent, consume, cossacks, crispy, crusades, cylinder, daringly, deceivers, decorates, depreciated, describing, deserts, desktop, detector, dictator, didgeridoo, difficult, diplomat, disclosed, dissent, dividends, dizzy, djibouti, dominant, droplet, economical, economy, editors, elkhound, emirates, emperor, emphasis, encumbered, engraver, enlivened, entries, epilogue, eritrean, exactly, examines, exmoor, explained, extreme, eyeless, facilitated, fairyland, fantasias, fastest, faulting, fermented, fervent, feudalism, feverfew, fibrous, fidelity, finalist, fishery, floppy, fluoride, flushes, forcibly, founding, freezing, frescoes, gargoyle, gavotte, geriatric, gingerbread, glandular, governed, grammars, granting, grateful, gravely, grisly, gristle, guangdong, hallelujah, handsets, hangover, happening, hartford, haughty, hibiscus, homestead, homilies, hornbill, hurry, igneous, illness, impudence, incisive, indicating, indonesia, infantile, infolding, inhibits, inorganic, insist, inspire, insured, interact, internee, invalids, irksome, january, jeweller, jugular, jumping, kestrel, kinetics, kirklees, labradors, lampeter, lancashire, legislate, leopards, lewisham, listing, literate, locust, lombardy, luxor, maintained, marathon, marksman, marshland, marvels, mascots, massaging, mayflies, meandering, meanwhile, mediation, megawatt, meiningen, membranes, mention, methodical, mimicry, missing, misused, mockery, mopping, morning, mosque, mosses, mouldy, moulted, mourned, muggins, muntjack, natives, negotiable, nightlife, nodules, nonchalance, norwich, observed, oncoming, opposed, ordering, oriented, osmium, outdated, overdue, oxygen, ozarks, pacifying, painting, pallbearer, pancreatic, panoramic, paraffins, paraguay, peacekeeper, pectoral, penrith, pensive, penumbra, pervades, pesticide, phonetic, pimples, pitcairn, platonic, plunder, polaroid, potent, powdered, practicable, praying, precedent, primula, privet, privy, proven, pulpy, quashes, quills, rancour, rational, raunchy, reality, recommend, redesigned, refrains, rejoicing, rejoins, relaxing, releasing, relying, remaining, repairer, reprise, resented, resist, retreads, revenue, revues, rework, rhesus, ringers, ringtail, royals, rummy, runner, rushes, rustic, rutland, sacrificial, sandown, sandwiched, saxifrage, schiphol, schisms, sculler, sectarian, secures, sellers, seminude, sensor, serenades, serrated, servile, shallow, sharpened, shelves, sheriffs, showy, siliconed, silting, siphoned, sister, sketches, skilful, slovakia, smashing, smooth, smyrna, snows, sought, soups, soviet, spheres, sphinx, spiders, splint, spoils, spying, stardom, stating, steroid, steward, stowage, strained, stuccoed, subheading, submerge, subotica, succeeding, suckles, suffolk, surgical, tapering, targets, tartaric, tasting, temples, tendency, termite, thatching, thunder, thwart, tibetans, tiensin, tomboy, tongkin, topper, toucher, towered, tracery, trackside, trailing, trident, tusks, twangy, tyrol, unbranched, unfused, unglazed, unless, unshared, uxbridge, variably, veganism, venerate, verbatim, vertical, vistas, vocally, waggoner, wallsend, warfarin, warring, whiting, wickets, windscale, winning, woomera, wording, worker, yerevan

Value 91

accompany, acoustic, acrobatics, adjutant, agitator, albumins, alleviated, ambulances, amulets, animator, announced, antecedent, apology, apparent, applause, appoint, aquatics, archaisms, archiving, asserted, assessed, assonance, asteroid, asylum, avengers, aviation, backsliding, baikonur, barefooted, battersea, battery, bilberry, bioassay, bisector, bolster, borrow, boulogne, bravery, brickmaker, brought, buccaneers, bullets, bussing, bypassed, calypso, canonized, canyons, carriers, castrated, cathedrals, cellophane, chancellor, chemically, childless, childwatch, chronicled, citation, closely, clutches, coalmines, coconut, compiler, compliance, concerns, conciliate, confidante, confining, conflicted, constable, content, corrected, couples, creature, crimson, custom, cyclist, damnation, dampness, darkness, debilitated, deception, deficiencies, delirium, democratic, dentist, deputy, derisive, despotic, detroit, discredit, dispense, disposed, divisible, doesburg, dogmatics, dowsing, drunkard, dubious, duvets, dynamite, dynamos, eastward, eisteddfod, electoral, eleventh, emancipated, emotion, endowing, enforcing, engagement, entailing, eradicating, escalating, eskimos, espionage, eunuchs, evaluated, evangelical, excelling, excerpt, exciting, exegetical, exerts, extends, extract, failures, fairness, fashions, fineness, fission, flexure, formulae, frailty, funnels, future, gangster, gardeners, genealogical, genealogy, genitive, gentleman, glaciation, grasping, greyish, grocery, growth, guests, habituated, hairless, hampering, harpist, harshly, hatters, heidelburg, heraldry, hesitated, hijackings, homelands, hominids, honour, idealistic, ideograms, impending, implicit, import, incidental, inclining, indulges, initiated, injecting, inlaying, interlaced, intimate, introduce, irishman, irrigated, issuer, kibbutz, lawless, layering, leftist, legality, legendary, lengthy, lentils, leveller, liberty, lifesize, lightpen, liquids, livery, lobster, longlegs, lovely, lovers, maestro, magnolias, malignant, manures, marriages, marshals, matadors, mayors, mazurka, meekness, megalomania, merrimack, metalloid, metering, microns, minerals, mirror, misguided, mobilize, modelling, modulate, monarchs, mortgagee, muppet, mythical, neutral, newborn, nipples, nitrated, noblesse, nominate, norfolk, noticing, objective, obtaining, occupies, offscreen, oilfields, olympia, oneness, opulence, origins, orphans, outraged, outreach, overland, pakistan, pamphlet, passive, pekingese, penitence, perform, phenomena, phoenix, pietism, pilots, pioneered, pistol, plaques, plaster, platelet, plenary, polecats, practise, prawns, prejudice, pretended, prison, private, probably, promenade, provable, psalter, puffins, pulley, pulling, purchase, qualify, quieten, radiation, rarity, realizable, rearranged, reasons, reclining, redefining, redirected, referent, regattas, regiment, regress, rejecting, relaunched, relaying, remarried, respond, retells, retrench, reunified, reverend, reviewed, rivers, rockets, rooming, rotifer, rounds, rumanian, safeguarded, sampling, santarem, sarajevo, satires, savings, schools, scrambler, sculpt, seafloor, segregated, sensual, shattr, sheathing, sherlock, shrunk, siblings, singers, sitter, skagerrak, slaloms, smelling, snappy, snowcap, sorts, spacetime, specifies, spherical, spirit, spoilt, spout, stamens, stapler, stills, striped, stuffs, subway, succumbed, sugary, surname, swamps, sweater, sweeper, sweeten, sweets, swings, switched, tabletop, talents, tannins, targetable, tattoo, tellers, tendons, tenors, theory, threaten, threats, thronged, tiananmen, tilting, touches, towns, trademark, trapeze, tricking, trivial, turku, tutelage, twist, typing, unbound, unequal, untried, unwise, urethra, vanity, varnish, vendetta, vertebra, vindicated, volley, walnut, warlord, washboard, weights, wetter, whilst, worlds, yearling

Value 92
abortive, abscesses, abstinence, accelerates, acclamation, adhesives, adjourned, adjuncts, adoptive, aftermath, airtight, alienating, although, altitude, ambergris amphibians, analyst, annoyance, antilles, appendices, appetite, applicant, aqueduct, arrives, artiste, ashtray, associate, attracted, audiotape, authored, automata, auxerre, bacterium, badminton, bathroom, billions, bismuth, blemishes, bletchley, bluebirds, blunter, blushing, bordering, braintree, brazilian, brightened, brushes, budgerigar, bulldogs, bureaux, buttock, button, calamities, calculus, captaincy, captors, cassette, castings, caucuses, cautioned, challenging, charities, charters, chartres, childbearing, circulate, civilised, claimants, clockmaker, colonies, commented, commercial, commits, commons, communal, compiles, complained, complies, contraband, cookery, corners, corpus, counts, couplet, crackdown, creditor, cricketer, crouches, crowns, crucibles, crumpled, cultish, debauchery, debutante, defendants, delegation, digestible, director, dismiss, disorder, divergence, donation, doubting, dreadlocks, drummer, duality, dustman, ecstasy, education, electron, eliminated, emanation, embassies, enamelling, encloses, enduring, ennobling, enshrine, entering, entrant, entreated, enunciate, episodes, equitable, escapist, established, estimate, exchanging, exempted, exercised, exigency, expects, extendable, falsity, fashionable, favoured,

federalism, fellows, feverish, fighters, fitness, flaccidity, focussed, followed, forested, formats, forties, fortified, forums, fostered, foundered, fracture, fragrances, fronts, germinate, gibraltar, gillingham, glorify, granaries, grandiose, grandson, granular, gravest, greenfly, greenwich, guarantee, gunfight, gypsy, handkerchief, harboured, heavenly, hegemony, hermits, hilltop, horrified, horror, hosting, hotelier, huskies, identify, ideological, ideology, immovable, impacting, implicated, incision, incurred, indelibly, indignant, infests, inflating, inherited, insatiable, inuits, inundated, invaders, inverse, israelis, issues, italianate, kerosene, kingdoms, labourer, lacrosse, latitude, laughter, learners, lectors, lemmings, licensing, liquified, liquor, livelier, livings, llanberis, longest, looting, lowers, luminance, luncheon, lurking, lynching, macclesfield, makeshift, manhattan, markings, meetings, memoirs, meridians, messianic, migrates, militias, milliner, minimum, minutiae, misjudged, mistaken, mistral, moorland, motets, mounted, mucous, muscles, nakedness, nantwich, nations, neurone, newhaven, nullified, numbers, obelisks, occasional, odours, offenders, offshore, ontario, opinion, oration, orgasms, ostrich, outcome, outlaw, pacemakers, partly, partner, pastels, penalized, pension, pentagon, periodical, pestered, petrified, phrasing, picture, plenty, plotted, policemen, porridge, porter, prefects, prevailed, probably, pulses, punching, purging, quakers, quarrel, quarto, quiver, racehorse, racialist, rajasthan, reasonable, rebellion, receiving, reckless, recoiling, refilling, refounded, relative, report, reserve, respite, restated, resting, retinue, reunite, reverse, revolt, rhythm, rickshaw, rioting, ripening, romping, rotten, sacrifices, salvador, sapphire, satirical, satisfied, sausages, savagely, scimitar, scourged, seafarers, seaplanes, seasons, seawater, segmented, senator, senescence, severance, shavers, shifting, shouted, shrews, shrines, simpler, skinny, sloping, slovene, slower, sockets, solidified, sounds, spacecraft, spores, stamper, staples, sticking, stones, strayed, stroked, struck, succinct, surfaces, sydney, tadpoles, tasmanian, telegraph, template, terminal, thinking, tightened, tingling, topsail, torts, totems, training, tramline, treason, trenches, tricycle, trucks, truro, tubingen, tucson, turns, tycoon, uncanny, undivided, unions, unison, unroll, unveiled, updating, urchins, valladolid, variegated, vehement, velingrad, vengeful, verandahs, vetoing, vigour, virginal, viscose, voucher, warmly, warthog, watery, wheelchair, whovian, wispy, withered, worried, wrexham, yearbook, yellow

Value 93
abridgment, abstracted, accentuate, accommodate, acquires, additives, admissible, aerobatics, ailerons, ailments, airshow, allergens, allowing, ambassador, amounted, anarchist, ancestral, annihilate, anthracine, appraisal,

approve, argentine, arrowhead, artefacts, aspiring, assault, astrakhan, attersee, audition, augury, auroras, auspices, baccalaureate, backwoods, ballerinas, baptismal, baroness, beginners, behavioral, bestowed, bisexual, bobsledding, bookshelf, borderland, bosnians, bottles, breakdown, breakout, bretons, brighton, bullfrog, capstone, carpeting, carvings, castaway, celluloid, censors, changeless, chariots, childbirth, chippenham, chlorides, chordates, churchmen, closest, closure, clumsy, cocktails, coloring, coloured, commanding, completed, compute, concerto, concordat, conformed, connects, conquer, convent, conveyed, copulate, covering, crucifix, cruiser, cubists, curries, curtailed, cyclopedia, deathwatch, deductive, deflection, dentifrice, desperate, detachment, detective, determine, dethroned, dialogues, didjeridoo, dieticians, discharges, disguise, disowned, disparate, disturb, dominion, dowries, dragoons, dripping, droopy, drought, drowns, dutiful, dwarfism, editorial, efficiencies, elements, elusive, encomium, encouraged, enquired, entity, entraps, ephesus, equally, equipped, erosive, errors, estranged, euphoria, exaggerate, exciseman, excludes, exegesis, eyebrow, facilities, factoring, fantastic, faversham, fifteenth, firmware, fisherman, fishguard, fistful, fixity, follicles, fragmented, freshly, friendly, fruits, galashiels, galloping, gittern, globules, goldfields, gospels, gotthard, gracious, granites, greenest, grimsby, growing, hamburger, handedness, harnessed, harrogate, harvest, hawsers, headlights, heraklion, heroines, holidays, hoopoes, horseman, housing, hundreds, hungarian, hungry, hunting, hurdling, ignoring, implodes, improbable, including, increases, indicator, inducers, infective, influenced, inhabiting, inherent, initials, inquire, intangible, internal, interred, invariable, invented, juniper, kathmandu, killings, kingship, knowing, lactifers, lancaster, landmarks, leisured, lesions, lessens, libraries, ligature, lightly, likewise, limiting, lioness, listeria, literacy, louvre, luckily, lyrebird, majesty, management, mandarins, marshalled, mastiffs, matchmaker, medication, melancholia, melanesian, midwest, milieux, militated, miscopied, misleading, mocassin, mummified, myrtle, nazareth, needlecraft, negligent, neonates, nihilism, notary, notifiable, nudity, nuggets, nuptial, objection, obsolete, officialdom, olympic, omnibus, outbreak, outlet, outside, pachyderm, pantheon, parachute, parents, parsnip, passion, payloads, penalty, pendants, persuaded, peterhof, photos, physical, pigmented, pinnacles, piston, pitiful, plaintiff, planting, platoon, playful, plucking, plugging, plunger, points, popping, porcelain, poster, praising, preachers, premiered, prickles, prizes, propaganda, provided, pupils, quarried, quotable, quotas, rankings, rapacity, rappers, rearguard, recesses, recording, rectifier, redolent, refuses, regulated, reinforce, reminding, remodelled, remorse, removable, reproof, require, retitled, revealing, rhapsodic, ringleader, robberies, romantic, rotunda, rulers, sailors, salicylic, samizdat, sarcastic, scanners, schizoid, screwy, sequenced, seventh, sextet, shearers, sherry, shingles, shortage, showcase, showman, shrapnel, side,slip, sighting, skaters, sloths, smallish, socialite, solenoid, sonatina, spewing, sprats, spreading, staining, stalking, stirred, stocky, stony, straps, streaks, stretch, strider, strive, strong, subpoena, suites, sumatra, sunbelt, sunny, swarms, syringa, tangerine, tangiers, tartans, tedious, tenants, terrier, testicle, theistic, therapy, thickener, thistle, threadlike, threefold, tinting, tissue, tolerance, tonight, torpedo, tours, trawls, triggered, trouble, trying, tucuman, tunicate, tunisia, uluru, unceasing, unchangeable, unfailing, unloved, unravel, untanned, untidy, uplifted, upstaged, urgency, uttered, vaguely, valletta, vapour, vassals, viennese, votive, voyager, wasting, weapons, weavers, widows, winkles, wisely, writer, yearning

Value 95
absolute, acquainted, actually, additions, adjustable, adrianople, aeronaut, alignment, allegorical, allegory, alligator, almighty, amenities, analogues, analyser, ancestor, ancillary, antedating, anthills, archipelago, armoured, arteries, assaying, assembles, attaining, attempt, axiomatic, baltimore, beaconsfield, berkshire, bespectacled, blanketing, blossom, blowfly, blunders, bombsight,

bookbinder, botswana, brainwash, bristol, browner, bulletin, busiest, byways, caernarfon, captives, carnation, carrying, cartilages, catabolism, catchword, ceremonial, chipmunk, choirboy, civilize, clavichord, clumping, coefficient, coexist, colonels, companies, conceives, concepts, concordance, confiscate, congolese, contacts, contains, convicted, corpses, coveting, craftsman, crayons, crooning, crossbar, currant, cynicism, dardanelles, decompose, deduction, delighting, democracies, dependency, depiction, depressed, detection, devaluing, devious, devotees, diacritics, dictation, diffusing, diglossia, directive, disarray, discover, dispensed, disperse, displayed, disposal, diverging, divorces, document, dordrecht, downgraded, draperiesm drawings, dressing, drivers, dumfries, duplicated, dynastic, edification, emergency, emphasise, employed, empress, enactment, enchanting, engulfing, epicentre, epileptic, erosion, establish, ethernet, ethically, euphoric, european, evenings, examples, explore, extinct, fanaticism, fastening, features, federative, feminist, fetuses, fictions, finishing, flavour, fledglings, flounder, foretold, founts, fraternal, freefalling, frisians, fullest, furnish, furrier, gentlemen, geometric, gesture, gigabytes, goalkeeper, gorgons, grammarian, grassland, gratings, gravesend, greatest, grotto, guangxu, guatemalan, guitars, hallmarks, halloween, harmless, haverhill, headphones, herbarium, hierarchical, hierarchy, holistic, honduran, housemaid, humankind, ideographic, illegally, immigrate, impatience, imperfect, impulse, inaccurate, incalculable, indefatigable, indefinite, infection, initialled, inspected, insult, interbred, intrepid, intruded, irishmen, kalamazoo, kindness, lactation, lamenting, lampooned, laryngeal, laundry, leakiness, libretti, limelight, lingering, liquefy, lisburn, lithuania, liveware, lubricated, lustre, magazines, malaysian, mallows, mangrove, martians, martyr, masques, masters, masticated, medallist, melancholic, meriting, meteors, migraines, millibars, misfits, mobilized, modulated, moisten, mollusc, monkfish, morpeth, mortlake, moulding, mustang, mutinied, mutism, mysore, nanterre,neolithic, nettles, nightmare, nightshade, nineties, nitrite, nominated, nonaligned, nucleus, nymphs, olfaction, olympiad, organize, painless, parishes, parkway, patents, peasants, pentagram, peppers, percolate, perishable, phoneme, phylum, pickups, pitfalls, pitting, pivotal, plethora, popery, practised, prairies, predictable, preference, preferred, pregnant, prejudiced, premium, prescribe, presides, priors, process, promise, proves, prudish, puffballs, pulping, punning, purchased, purify, quieter, quirks, ragworm, ranters, rationale, rattles, readymades, reaffirms, reasoner, receipts, recovered, refashion, relaxant, relieves, relishes, renewing, renounce, repeating, resort, respected, result, retailing, retaliated, retracing, reverence, richness, ripples, risings, robust, rodents, romeo, romsey, rounder, sabotaging, saloons, sanction, scattered, scavenges, scholars, scooter, screwball, sedition, serums, shoemaker, showing, sicilians, simony, sixpence, skunks, skyline, slackening, slavonic, slipper, slotted, snorted, solway, sorry, spaniels, sparking, speedily, spinner, splits, sponges, spooks, spouse, sprung, staircase, starlike, staying, steadily, stiller, stopped, stout, strands, streams, subdivide, summit, summon, supper, surging, surnamed, sweeter, terracing, textile, thickest, thickets, thinning, throbbing, trackers, tractor, tradesman, trekking, tribute, tricycle, troupe, tubular, tuesday, turbans, ulster, unguarded, unholy, unlocks, upholds, usurp, utrecht, uvular, vandalism, vaults, victims, vinegars, virtue, wandering, warrant, waspish, wayward, weevils, welcomes, welshman, wexford, whisky, wholly, whorls, winchcombe, wingers, wisest, wishbone, workman, worst, wroclaw, zigzags

Value 96
abolishing, abrasives, accounts, activism, advocating, agitation, airbrush, airways, alternate, analyses, anchovies, animation, antipope, appliances, apprehended, aptitude, aquifers, armpits, assembly, assisted, associated, augsburg, automate, averting, azerbaijani, background, barbarity, barnsley, battering, battlefield, bigotry, blasters, blowzy, boulders, brewery, burying, buxton, calibrating, cantonese, capsules, carcinomas, celebrating, cerebellum, characters, chequers, chimneys, cincinnati, circulated,

cockpits, coincident, colossal, commencing, commoner, comparing, compatible, concludes, confederate, conjugate, considered, contest, convener, costume, councils, counter, courts, cruelly, crusading, curator, cyclones, czarist, daylength, decorating, delicately, delocalized, demeanour, density, desegregate, destiny, devoting, diaphragms, dignities, directly, disciples, doctrinal, doomsday, draftsman, dwindling, economics, eindhoven, electrified, emblematical, employee, engineers, enshrined, entrenched, enunciated, episcopal, equalize, estimated, eventing, examining, exhibits, exists, expires, facsimiles, factories, faculties, falmouth, fascists, favorite, february, fixative, floggings, flooring, flushing, flywheel, fondness, fonthill, forgiven, fractured, freeholder, freemason, fribourg, frightened, funerals, further, galloway, gearboxes, germinated, glosses, goatskin, graduates, grenadines, gripping, groups, guaranteed, guildford, harassing, hatcheries, helpless, hesitant, homeless, hormonal, however, hoxton, humour, hydrogen, icebreakers, idealizing, identifiable, idiolects, imittes, immutable, imparts, imposes, indicative, injures, innuendo, insincere, installed, intending, invariance, invoices, ionizer, jacuzzi, keyless, knowledge, knuckles, lacquers, leicester, lethargy, linearly, logically, lorries, loudest, lovesick, lumberjack, machinery, machinist, manifested, martello, masseur, matters, metaphor, minefields, moldovan, monogram, morally, moribund, mouths, mustard, muster, naivety, narrates, naughty, neglecting, negotiate, newcomer, nightclub, norway, numerical, nurses, obstacles, organism, oscillate, outboard, outline, overcome, overheard, ovulate, oxidized, paignton, panelist, panpipes, parallels, parasitic, parsley, parsonage, paupers, pavement, peanuts, pennines, performance, perinatal, peroxide, pervading, pictured, playboy, players, poignant, poppies, portico, postcard, potty, powers, primeval, primus, printa, proceeding, proclaimed, procure, projected, psychical, published, pumping, punished, purism, quadrant, quasars, rations, realistic, recoinages, recycling, reliving, repulse, rescuing, reserved, resolve, retort, retreated, return, reunion, reunited, reversed, rhetoric, rhombus, rosary, rushing, samaritan, satanism, scaffolding, schedules, scorching, seagulls, securing, segmental, semicircle, sexist, sheltered, shoots, sidelines, signifier, sixteen, sketching, skirts, slimming, sloops, snapping, snowy, soberly, sociall, society, solicited, sounder, spaceship, spidery, spongy, spools, sprains, sprint, stagings, stagnant, stalemate, stamford, steamboat, stickleback, stores, subarctic, suckers, suckling, summing, swearing, swifts, synods, teapots, tenement, tension, theatres, thermals, thetford, thirdly, tolerate, torque, trieste, trimmer, trolls, truly, turbot, turner, turtle, unadorned, unalienable, unearthed, uniform, unmanageable, unofficial, unrefined, unsung, utopian, valleys, varying, vertebrae, vertigo, vibrates, volatile, vowels, walkway, whiplash, whistle, whitish, whoever, wicklow, windmill, windpipe, windward, witney, wolves, woollen, wounds, wrinkled, wrongs, zimbabwean

Value 98
abrasions, abridgement, accelerating, accessibly, acrimony, addictions, adjuster, adolescent, affections, affinities, amateurs, amidships, analytical, antibodies, anticipate, anxiety, anything, apolitical, appreciated, arouses, arriving, assizes, attackers, azimuth, blacklisted, blindness, blizzard, bookmaking, boyfriend, bromeliads, buoyant, burglars, buzzard, capability, carbonates, causeway, ceremony, champions, chemnitz, cheshunt, chichester, chinchillas, chivalry, civilians, clergyman, clippers, cluster, coalition, coarsely, coastline, cohorts, commandant, comoros, compiling, comprise, condemning, condenses, confluence, contagion, contender, copious, cornwall, corporal, county, cremation, criminals, cripples, crockery, cropping, crosses, crouching, crystal, culminate, deciphering, degradation, deliverance, deliverer, democrats, dendrites, deprives, despots, detergent, dettingen, develops, dialysis, diphtheria, diplomacy, disagreeing, disappeared, disputed, distinct, draughts, drooping, dualistic, dunstable, dwellers, dynamism, economies, elaborates, elevator, elongates, embankment, embroidered, enclosing, endorser, entrails, enveloped, epidermis, equalling, everglades,

excision, exhaust, explicit, export, eyesight, fabrication, falsetto, fibreglass, financiers, fisheries, fixation, flowers, foreplay, forlorn, formulaic, gemstone, geysers, glycerine, goodness, grammatical, grooming, grounds, guardsman, gunners, harshest, heathrow, herrings, highbury, histamine, honeybees, hostels, hovering, humanism, idealists, immaculate, impinging, improve, incunabula, independence, indication, indifference, infamous, inferences, infertile, inflexible, informer, inhabitant, inscribes, insulin, invested, invites, isomers, istanbul, ivanovo, jewelry, jointing, juvenile, kirghizia, kittens, latrines, latvians, levelling, liaisons, lifetimes, lighters, listens, lonesome, loophole, marigolds, marketing, marquis, marzipan, massacres, materials, medugorje, memorabilia, menswear, microfilm, migrating, militant, minimize, mission, modifiers, montreal, moonlit, morbidly, morphine, mortals, mothers, municipal, murders, narrowed, natures, nostalgia, novocaine, nozzle, oblivion, occasions, officially, oligarchical, oligarchy, originate, osprey, overlay, panegyric, panoramas, parchment, partisan, partridge, pavilion, piquant, pitchrs, plainchant, ploughs, postman, potency, powys, prepares, primers, principal, profess, prompt, prophet, proton, provence, proxy, prudent, python, quenching, quickly, rallying, raucous, realities, recommenced, references, reformer, regenerate, rehearses, remembers, renowned, repelling, reprieve, resembles, rewrite, rheumatic, roentgen, rooting, rotates, routes, rybinsk, sacrificing, saleroom, sanatoria, savagery, scandalized, scarcity, scooping, scrambling, scrolls, sectional, seminars, sequels, sheepdogs, shellfish, shipping, shorebird, shrinks, simplex, simplon, sinners, sitting, snowball, softens, solving, somebody, somehow, soprano, speedway, spilling, spoons, sprawled, sprays, squabbles, squeeze, starboard, station, stevenage, stocking, stoning, strut, stumped, subscribe, subsides, suburban, sufferer, suggest, sunset, surfacing, suspend, swaying, sweating, sweeping, swindon, swords, symbolic, tablecloth, tampons, tarnished, tashkent, tellings, tempest, tendencies, theocracy, thermos, thrown, together, transcend, tremolo, triassic, trust, tumbling, turnip, tyrant, ukrainian, unchanging, uncover, uneducated, valuers, vegetables, venison, vicious, villains, vineyard, virgins, virginia, visits, wallasey, warblers, wardship, warrens, wastrel, waterfall, wetlands, wetting, whisper, whitehall, winsome, wintered, wonders, yangtze, yours, zealots, zygote

Value 99
aborigines, accompanies, accomplices, accomplish, acquiring, addressees, adirondacks, airships, amalgamating, ambivalent, amritsar, anodizing, answers, anthracite, anywhere, aphorism, apologies, appearances, appenines, aqueous, archbishop, ardently, arduous, argument, aromatics, artistic, ascension,

ascertained, assigning, attndant, autocrat, axolotl, banquets, bastions, batteries, bellowing, bestiary, bibliophile, biographer, bishopric, bloomers, blotting, bottling, bronzes, brothels, bruising, bursts, caissons, camcorders, cancerous, caricature, carnivals, celebrity, cellulite, certificate, channelling, chihuahuas, civilized, coalhouse, collateral, colliery, colonize, competence, conducts, confederacy, confiscated, congregated, consented, consist, conspire, container, cordially, corsets, courser, craftsmen, crampons, crawlers, creators, creditably, crenellated, criticised, croquet, crushing, culprit, cupboards, curative, current, dazzling, decomposed, decorator, delusion, demographic, deputies, deviation, diagnosing, diagrammatic, digitally, discharging, disdainful, disgust, dispersed, dissented, divisive, doncaster, drifters, dropping, drumming, dyslexia, eccentrics, egocentric, electrician, elliptical, emphasised, encumbrance, endearment, enjoying, enthralled, entrances, entrapped, eradication, ergonomic, erupts, escalation, escorts, euthanasia, evergreen, excesses, excluding, exhorted, explored, expound, external, eyelashes, facetious, fallacious, federalist, filaments, fingerboard, firsthand, fittest, florist, folksong, forelimbs, forsook, fortune, fossils, fractional, fruity, fugitive, genealogies, generally, geocentric, geomagnetic, ghoulish, gigantism, goodnight, gourmet, gritty, groceries, grunts, gunboats, gymkhanas, gymnast, habitation, heartbeats, hcctoring, heliograph, hexameter, hitters, hopeless, hornets, hosiery, hourly, humanely, ilchester, illinois, immigrated, impartial, impermeable, impress, imprint, incipient, incoherence, increasing, indecisive, indemnify, inevitable, inflecting, injection, inputs, insisted, integrate, intricate, invaluable, invincible, involve, isotope, judgement, kilobyte, labouring, landlords, landslides, letters, liability, liberalize, liberties, limericks, lipstick, lisieux, lucknow, lunatics, mainframes, maintenance, malignancy, manually, marmots, mayotte, mentioned, minarets, modality, moments, monoxide, neighbour, nutmegs, nylons, oculist, offerings, officiated, openings, operates, oporto, organized, orogeny, outcast, overcoat, pastry, patriot, payroll, pedology, peerless, penury, percolated, physics, planners, plastics, plundered, plurals, poetry, popular, pouncing, premiss, prescribed, prestige, promised, propagate, prosodic, pruning, ptarmigan, purest, puritan, pyramidal, quadrille, qualifies, quimper, ransoms, rapture, rarities, reactors, readmitted, reappears, rebirths, recipient, recommended, reflecting, refusing, rejection, renounced, reoccupied, repudiate, resisted, reviver, revolve, rewarding, rightly, rollers, roughing, sargasso, satisfy, savannahs, saxhorn, scorning, scrapers, sectors, seniors, servant, settler, severing, sharply, shavings, shorten, shorts, sickness, significance, situated, sixths, skegness, sleepers, slovaks, slowing, sneezing, snowman, solidify, sometime, spasmodic, spindly, splashes, spotted, stamping, startled, stilts, stinging, strewn, stricken, strove, strung, subdivided, subjects, subsidy, subtly, surgeon, sycamore, synapse, syrup, szechwan, tactitians, tactless, taverns, telepathic, tentacles, theories, thirteen, thought, thrones, thwarted, thyroid, titbits, tonally, toughened, tradesmen, travelled, triples, tripoli, tuneful, unmarked, unburned, underside, undertake, unfactual, unreliable, untrue, upholder, upright, validating, vanities, vastly, vaulter, vehicular, viaducts, vocation, voters, warmest, wasteland, whipsnade, wickedest, windspeed, withhold, workload, workmen, worry, wryneck, zealous

Value 102
abbotsford, adaptogens, advancement, aesthetes, affiliation, aldershot, aleutians, allocation, ambitions, amorous, anaesthesia, analysing, anglicanism, antibiotic, anticipated, antonym, approaches, assimilable, attracts, auditioned, authors, autistic, axillary, bandicoots, banister, battledore, benevolence, benzedrine, biscuits, bookbinding, brentford, brixton, broadcasts, browning, buccaneering, bullying, butchery, cabinetmaker, californian, calvinism, castanets, casualty, catalepsy, catchphrase, categories, cemeteries, charioteer, chequebook, chernobyl, choosers, circuits, cleverly, collapses, colonnades, comments, committed, competing, complacent, comprised, concerning, concertina, concluding, configured, conquered, coolness,

correctable, cowboys, coyotes, criticize, critique, culminated, cyprus, declaration, decorative, deprecating, deregulated, desiccation, developer, digestion, dimension, diplomatic, discerning, discourage, disendowed, disfigured, dishonor, disposable, disproof, district, disturbed, downward, dragonfly, duration, ecumenism, elections, emphasize, emulating, englishman, enhancement, equation, evocative, exerting, exorcised, expedient, expiring, extending, fashioning, fatalities, favours, ferrous, flashbulbs, flintlock, floribunda, flutter, follows, footballs, forefather, forests, forgeries, formally, founders, foundling, framlingham, freezers, function, generalize, geographical, geography, girlfriend, glottis, goldfinches, graduating, grandfather, gravelly, gravity, grosses, halesowen, handicapping, harbours, hardships, harmonies, harvested, haymarket, henceforth, herbivore, homecoming, humiliated, hundredth, ichneumon, ideographs, imitating, imposing, impregnable, improved, impudent, incapacitate, incendiary, ineffectual, inherits, injuring, inkblots, interdict, initially, intimacies, intricacy, intuited, jumpers, laburnum, landforms, lecturer, legalizing, legations, leinster, leninist, lionheart, liquidated, listener, locational, loyally, luckless, lymphoid, magnesium, mainstay, malicious, manifesto, mastercard, matchwood, meaningful, meditating, mentally, mercenary, minimized, modifying, monkeys, mothballs, mounts, mulatto, mummers, murderer, mutiny, mystical, narcotics, narrating, nashville, neanderthal, necrosis, negatives, newcastle, nitrogen, nonlinear, nowadays, nursing, obscures, ombudsman, optional, ordinances, originated, outcry, outward, oyster, pacifists, painters, parodist, parsons, pastimes, pastoral, permeates, pictogram, piloting, platemaker, plaudits, pneumatic, polarize, polisher, prayers, precepts, prefixes, pretoria, prevails, princely, principle, prolapse, promote, province, provoke, puppies, puppy, quantock, quartet, quilter, ragwort, randomly, rapidity, reasoning, recension, recently, reognize, recondense, reflector, regenerated, regretted, relandscaped, reluctance, reprieved, residency, resigning, retrieve, riposte, riverbeds, ropemaker, rorqual, rosette, rounding, routine, runway, russet, salesgirl, sandpiper, scheduling, schooling, scratching, seapower, segments, selection, serengeti, shepherds, shetlands, shoemaking, shoeshine, shoulder, shrimps, shuffling, sidelining, simplified, slavery, slipping, sluggish, smuggler, snowfall, softener, solstice, sorbonne, sorting, sparring, specialised, specially, speculate, spinning, spitfire, spoleto, springs, squeezed, stallion, stansted, stately, steeply, storey, storing, storks, straddles, straight, stranger, strategic, strays, stretched, submarine, subscribed, subsonic, suburbs, suitor, sulphate, supplied, swinging, technique, tenures, theocratic, thousand, threshes, thriller, timeless, toolkit, torpedoed, trailers, triennial, trombone, trophy, troyes, tureens, turret, uncouth, underline, unfolding, unhindered, unhurt, unwanted, upstate, upwards, utilize, valentine, validity, vectors, vegetarian, version, vibrating, vintner, violets, warrior, weighting, welwyn, whatever, whirligig, windsor, winners, woodbridge, woolly, wreckers, wrestle

Value 103
abandonment, aberration, abstracts, acidification, activist, admiralty, admission, advertise, algorithm, allegories, allusion, altimeter, ameliorated, amounts, analyzes, anointing, anteaters, anxious, aphrodisiac, apocrypha, aquatint, asparagus, asphyxia, assemblages, assuming, astounded, atrophy, austrian, automatic, autumnal, aversion, ayrshire, backwaters, balustrade, bankrupt, baritones, baronetcy, bestows, betrayals, biarritz, biennially, biochemist, bloodless, bolivians, bolshevik, bookkeeper, brazenly, britanny, brusque, budgetary, byelarus, calculating, camouflages, canvasses, capitalism, captures, carefully, caricatured, carnforth, castleford, catapulted, causation, centrepiece, chartering, chelmsford, chertsey, cinemascope, circumcise, cleansings, clownish, coincidences, collector, colonized, colours, committee, communes, complaint, condition, conforms, connaught, consecrate, conspired, consular, consuls, contracted, convening, conveys, corporeal, counting, coupons, crinolined, criticism, crocodiles, crossbred, crowning, culinary, daughters,

decelerating, definitive, demarcation, dependencies, deserving, designates, detonates, diffusion, discussed, dispersal, dissident, dissonance, distracted, dromedary, ductless, elevation, elizabethan, embossing, emergencies, emigrating, emission, enlightened, enslaving, enthroned, equilibria, evaporate, everyman, expanses, exposes, fastness, favourable, fieldwork, firmness, fixture, fomenting, footwear, foreseeing, foundry, fragments, freeholding, freeport, frosty, generator, gestural, glossop, gravedigger, gravitate, grievances, groningen, gruesome, grumbling, guerrilla, gunroom, hamsters, handicrafts, handiwork, heliport, hierarchies, hitherto, hustler, imperilled, impetus, incubator, infesting, infighting, inflicting, inhalation, integrated, intrigue, invasion, involved, ionizing, ironware, irrawaddy, jesuits, justified, juvenilia, lanterns, lawyers, lectures, leprechaun, lesbianism, lessons, liquefies, liqueur, litters, logarithm, loosely, lowering, lymphoma, maturing, meadowlark, melatonin, merciless, mercury, millions, miscarriage, molasses, mongoose, motives, muskrat, mutton, muzzle, natterjack, newsboy, nonverbal, numbering, numerals, nuremberg, nystadt, obvious, officious, opulent, organist, otranto, overcast, overdose, oversaw, overseen, palaeozoic, paradoxes, paraphrase, particles, patrons, patterned, penicillin, penitent, pennants, perfecting, perfumes, perspex, pessary, pheasants, phenomenal, pictorial, pidginized, pigments, pilgrims, plankton, pogroms, polishes, politics, polyps, pregnancy, princess, privilege, profits, propagated, propelled, publicize, pundits, purist, quartz, quavers, rancidity, rapacious, readership, realists, reappearance, reassembled, receptive, recruited, removing, reopening, repellant, repudiated, retargeted, revising, revolved, roadshow, roasting, rotting, rousing, runaway, runcorn, rusty, satellite, scantily, scenarios, seasoning, seizure, semantics, september, sermons, sextant, shorter, showboat, slandering, socialized, socorro, soldering, sorcery, sounding, souring, spacious, spawning, specimens, spectacles, splendor, squalor, stabilize, stencilled, stimuli, stitches, student, stunted, subatomic, subdeacons, sundays, suspect, sustain, swampland, swastika, syntax, tallahassee, taoists, temperate, textual, theorems, throws, tossing, treachery, treeless, triggers, troops, truest, trunks, turning, tuscany, tutored, umbrellas, unacceptable, unachievable, undergone, undermine, unfederated, ungainly, unleavened, unmarried, vampires, vanishing, vertebral, videowall, virtual, vividly, walkout, watchmaker, watershed, waveform, whiskies, willesden, wingspan, wordbook, worsened, yodelling, zepellin

Value 107
aboriginals, accounting, accretions, acrostics, acuteness, advertised, advisors, aeronautic, afterbirth, agnostics, agreements, albatross,

alcoholism, alexandrine, amalgamation, ambiguity, amerindians, anglophone, antelopes, anticlerical, apostles, apprentice, atonement, auditors, auotcracy, autograph, avowedly, ballrooms, biometry, bombardment, bookstall, browsing, butchering, cauldrons, celebrities, certainly, chinatown, churchward, cigarettes, circumcised, cisterns, classicism, clustered, collieries, colonist, conferences, connector, conniving, consecrated, considerable, contradict, conveyance, copyist, coroners, courting, cultivable, currency, custody, denudation, deploying, deposits, dignitary, disadvantage, discordant, disneyland, disqualified, doctrines, dovetails, dressers, earthquake, embolisms, emplacement, engineering, enquirer, ensuring, envisaging, enzymes, epilepsy, especially, ethology, evangelism, evaporated, excellences, excrement, exercises, exhausted, exhibiting, existing, expenses, experts, exported, extents, faintness, fatalists, flattery, flightpath, foresight, formless, fourths, foxhound, fragility, franciscans, frankness, frictional, frigidity, fructose, genotype, geraniums, glasnost, glycerides, goldsmith, gorgeous, grouping, guadeloupe, happiness, hardwoods, hawthorn, haystacks, heartburn, helsingor, hepatitis, hercegovina, hiberenating, highlights, hindwings, hoodlums, hopscotch, hormones, horsetail, hottest, household, hyacinths, imparting, impatient, impeachment, implement, inductive, infantry, inflection, infringing, infuriated, infusion, intrigued, inverts, irreplaceable, isotherm, justly, khartoum, killarney, kilmarnock, konigsberg, landmasses, libellous, liberalist, limehouse, littoral, llandrindod, logograms, lollipop, longitude, lymphatic, mauritania, measuring, medicinally, microfilmed, military, minidisks, minister, minnows, modalities, monograph, monrovia, monthly, moralist, mormons, mountain, movement, mullingar, multimedia, navigator, neapolitan, neutron, numbness, omitting, onerous, openness, optimum, orchestra, overseer, overtime, painkiller, palindrome, palliative, pangolins, paraphrased, paraplegics, parrots, patriarchal, peepshow, personable, pharyngeal, photons, pianists, plainsong, ploughman, plovers, poisons, pompoms, portion, powering, pragmatics, precincts, pressing, preston, previewed, printing, privileged, producing, professed, programs, prompted, prosper, provider, puberty, publicized, punishable, putting, pyrenees, quantum, radioactive, rarifying, rationing, ravishing, rearwards, recapture, receptacles, recession, rededication, reductive, reflection, refractive, refreezes, relational, repeaters, repellent, researching, retailers, reverent, reverts, rigours, rookery, rosebush, sacramental, salamanders, sanitary, sanitized, satirize, sawdust, schenectady, scuppered, secretly, semifinals, semitism, sepulchre, shooting, shorthand, showers, skimmers, skirting, smothered, snatchers, socialist, software, solidifies, solvent, songbirds, sparkling, sports, sprocket, squatted, stabilized, statehood, stationed, stavanger, stettin, stoicism, stowing, striking, stripped, strokes, studios, sturdy, subsidies, subvert, suggested, sultanas, superman, suspended, sussex, swimming, syllables, tabulating, technocrat, telephonic, telescopic, tenacious, teutonic, theological, theology, thriving, thrower, tilbury, timezone, tireless, titanium, tottered, transcended, trapdoor, treasure, trolley, trooper, truffles, trumps, trusted, tunisian, twenty, twickenham, uncovered, undeniably, underdogs, underlies, undermined, uninhabited, unitarian, unlimited, unlucky, unquiet, unratified, unreason, unrecorded, unskilled, unspeakable, upsurge, utterance, vermont, visions, vitamins, volumes, walsingham, wanderers, waterhole, waterline, wavelets, weaverbird, werewolf, whooping, windows, woodlands, woodwind, worries, wounding

Value 113
aberdeenshire, abnormally, abortions, absurdist, adversary, advisory, alertness, almsgiving, almshouse, altruism, aluminium, amphibious, antagonism, apartness, apocalypse, apparatus, appreciates, aquaplaning, arboretum, asthmatics, attracting, auditory, automobile, avuncular, battalions, bedfordshire, benefactions, biometrics, blazonry, bodywork, boosters, bootlegging, breadwinner, broadcasting, bywaters, catapults, categorized, centralize, chiropody, circuiting,

cleanliness, coagulants, commenting,
compendium, conductor, constanza, constrain,
consulted, contracts, convoys, covenants,
cultivate, cuttings, debentures, decisively,
demagnetized, derbyshire, desecration, deserters,
discourse, dishonest, dispirited, disputes,
dissenter, disservice, dissimilar, distress,
dreamworld, dressmaker, easterlies, economist,
eliminating, elucidation, encyclopaedia,
endowment, entropy, escalators, esperanto,
ethnicity, euphrates, exceedingly, excretion,
exercising, exorcist, expediting, explorer,
exponent, exudation, fairground, favouring,
festivals, festoons, flucuated, flummery,
focussing, following, formalist, fostering,
freshness, frontline, fruitful,gasworks,
genetically, glassmaking, hagiographer,
harmonized, harrowing, hazardous, headmasters,
headstreams, hemispheric, hereditary, herniation,
historian, homeopathic, hyperbolic, illuminance,
imprison, incurring, indemnity, indulgences,
inferiors, infidelity, infirmary, ingenious,
inheriting, innocents, inquiry, inseminated,
insouciance, intestate, intolerable, introduced,
invariably, jeopardized, judgments, kilimanjaro,
knockabout, latterly, laundress, laxatives, layouts,
libertines, lifestyle, lightness, linearity, liveliest,
longshore, loyalist, luminary, mackintosh,
magistrate, magnitudes, mainstream,
manwatching, marquess, marseilles, masterly,
maximums, mesolithic, methodist, methylated,
mezzanine, miscellany, modernied, modestly,

monitored, moonlets, moonlight, morality, mounting, mutation, neoclassical, nonstop, normalize, nourished, novelty, nullity, occupying, omission, operation, optically, optimize, organizer, originally, ornamental, output, overlook, overrun, pangbourne, pantomimic, pathways, patriarchs, patterns, payments, penniless, percentages, perennials, perjury, persevere, pertaining, perverted, pineapples, pinpoint, plotting, polewards, porpoise, portray, potters, prediction, premarital, prevailing, prevalent, primness, primrose, procedural, projectile, protest, provenance, pugilist, pulpits, punters, puppets, qualities, quantify, quarrelled, quiescent, razorbill, rearrested, recompense, recruits, recurring, referential, relations, renderings, residents, resistance, resister, resonances, restrained, rivalries, roughcut, rustler, saarbrucken, sacraments, salvation, sartorial, satsumas, scavengers, scholarly, scottish, scruples, seaports, senility, separator, servicemen, settings, seychelles, shallower, shareholder, shepherding, shouting, simplest, sinister, skippers, slowest, smoother, solidity, soundboard, spacesuit, specialist, specifying, spellings, splinter, spokesman, spotter, springing, spurts, squirted, sternly, straying, stroking, struggled, strummed, stunts, subeditor, submitted, subtracted, successes, surgery, surpass, swimmer, syndrome, systemic, terrors, texture, theodolite, tightening, tiredness, topically, transcribed, transglobe, trappers, traveller, truants, trumpet, turntable, tutors, twitching, typhoon, unbeliever, undertaken, unilateral, uninflected, universe, unmusical, unrewarded, unsuited, unwieldy, uprising, upstream, urinating, vagueness, vaudeville, vietnamese, viruses, warships, watermill, westward, willows, wincanton, withering, worldwide, worsens

Value 114
abergavenny, abundantly, accordingly, accompanist, activation, admonition, adulteries, adventist, afflictions, aggression, agrochemicals, alignments, alligators, amounting, ampleforth, ancestors, annulment, apologist, articulated, astonished, attempts, ayatollahs, beatification, behavioural, benevolent, binoculars, blossoms, bluebottle, bookseller, borrower, botanically, bulletins, capricious, carnations, casualness, catchwords, centralism, centuries, ceremonials, chesterfield, choirboys, choreograph, chrysalis, classicist, clumsily, coefficients, colouring, completing, conception, confessor, conforming, confronted, conjecture, conquest, constancy, continent, contorted, contrary, converging, conveying, coppermine, cornishman, cottesloe, courgette, courtly, crossbow, cumbersome, currants, curtailing, customer, darlington, decomposes, deductions, deliberation, depictions, dereliction, desolation, determinate, directorial, disasters, discounted, discovers, disperses, distorted, divisional, documents, domination, dyspepsia, efficiently, elocution, embroidery,

empiricism, enactments, encompassed, encouraging, encyclopedic, endeavoured, enlargement, enquiring, equipping, equivalence, escarpment, europeans, evangelist, excavation, executive, explores, extenders, exterior, fairweather, feminists, fertilized, fingernails, fishmonger, flagellation, flavours, flounders, footholds, foreshadow, frequency, frostbite, genealogist, gestures, goalkeepers, governor, grammarians, grasslands, greensward, guayaquil, guernsey, harnessing, historical, history, holocaust, honorary, horoscope, hydration, identically, illiteracy, illnesses, importance, importer, impulses, inclusive, indentured, indivisible, infections, infiltrate, influencing, innumerable, insults, intensified, inventing, isolation, jottings, justifiable, keystone, literally, lithograph, lustres, magisterial, manoeuvre, martyrs, masterpiece, matrilineal, megavitamin, melodramatic, mesmerism, mesopause, microlight, moderation, molluscs, momentum, mouldings, muezzin, munificent, nationwide, nervous, newtown, nightmares, nineteenth, nutcracker, optimism, organizes, ormskirk, orthopaedic, overlapped, partially, performance, performer, permanency, perpetual, persuading, phonetician, picaresque, polygamy, posture, precocity, preferences, premiums, prescribes, princeton, prisoner, problematic, promises, prophecies, prostate, protocol, providing, proviso, purloined, putative, quakerism, raindrops, reasserted, recitation, reclusive, regulating, rehabilitated, relaxants, rcluctant, remodelling, replicating, requested, reorts, responder, results, retitling, rhapsodies, rheumatoid, rotterdam, rounders, sacristy, sanctions, schoolboy, secretary, senatorial, sequencing, shoemakers, shrewdly, shrivelled, signature, silicosis, sixtieth, smallness, snowdonia, somerset, soundbox, sovereign, sphinxes, spinners, spitting, spouses, staircases, stalwart, starlets, starlight, steersman, stirring, stockpiled, straggling, strangler, stranraer, stumpy, sturdier, subsidize, summits, summons, swallowed, sweetener, swiftly, synagogue, syntactic, tajikistan, taxonomic, textiles, theorist, thermally, thermionic, throwing, timekeeping, tormented, tractors, translated, transmit, tributes, triumphed, trooping, troupes, turnpike, twister, undergoing, undeterred, unhealthy, unionism, uplifting, uprooted, uruguay, uttering, valparaiso, virtues, waitress, wanderings, warmonger, warrants, westmeath, whistler, whitsun, windermere, wintery, workforce, workwear, worthing, wrongly, yoghurt

Value 155

accountability, administrative, authenticity, authoritarian, bacteriologist, carnivorous, christianity, cinematography, computerized, consciously, conscription, consequential, conservation, conspicuous, constipation, consultancies, contemplative, contentious, continuation, contrapuntal, contributor, conversation, copiousness, decompression, determinists, differentiation, discriminative, distinctions, distributor, enthusiasts, explicitness, figuratively, fingerprints, geophysicist, historicity, hydrobiology, hydrocephalus, immortality, incongruity, intercollegiate, interpreting, interviewing, irrepressible, isolationism, leatherworks, leicestershire, malabsorption, millionairess, multiparty, neurologist, outbursts, phosphorus, photometry, plausibility, possibility, postscript, precipitation, prerogatives, professions, progression, prohibitory, propulsion, prosecution, proverbially, pyrotechnics, rationalizing, registration, scurrilous, showjumping, simplification, songwriting, stylistics, substantiated, suggestions, supplication, supporting, teleconferencing, troposphere, trumpeters, ultraviolet, underwriter, unfortunate, unvanquished, viceroyalty, vitrification, walthamstow, welterweight

Value 160
adventurous, appropriating, assassination, astronautics, authentication, bloodlessness, carburettors, classificatory, comparatively, complementary, computational, conclusively, constituent, contribution, dehumanization, distribution, distrusting, electrocution, embryologist, evangelization, expenditures, exploitation, extensively, fastidiously, futurology, heterosexism, hybridization, hypothesized,

impersonating, incrementation, influentially, inseparability, instructive, interrelation, intertropical, investments, luxurious, manufacturers, microcircuits, microgravity, municipalities, neighbourhoods, observatory, orthodontics, perpetuation, perspiration, perversions, philosophers, polyurethane, prescriptive, preservative, pressurized, principalities, purifications, repository, roundworms, saxophonist, sequentially, servomotor, shortcomings, stereoscopy, stonecutter, strengthening, stringfellow, subconscious, substituted, superimposed, supplements, suprasensible, surmounts, surrounding, sympathizer, thoroughbreds, tournaments, townspeople, traditionlly, transports, tribulations, troglodytes, trusteeship, typecutting, typesetting, unpleasantly, versatility, voraciously

Value 161
administrator, antihistamines, behaviouristic, bioluminescent, bipartisanship, compositional, consultative, countersunk, dictatorships, electronvolt, epistemology, exceptionally, externalities, fluctuations, frustration, grasshoppers, inconsistent, indestructible, ineffectiveness, insubstantial, interpretive, irresponsible, liverworts, lymphocytes, multinational, nonfigurative, nonsporting, omnidirectional, omnivorous, oppositional, ornamentalist, orotundity, overlordship,

parturition, perfunctory, philologists, polytheistic, portraiture, precociously, preconditions, presbyteries, promulgation, proprietary, prosperity, radiofrequency, recommissioned, sharecroppers, spectroscopic, subcutaneous, subordination, subversives, supportive, supranational, suprematist, surrealists, technologically, teleprinters, temperatures, terrorists, thoroughfares, transantarctic, translocation, triangulation, undercurrent, undifferentiated, unilateralist, unimportant, voiceprinting, voluminous, weightlifters, wholeheartedly, wirecutters, yourselves

Printed in Great Britain
by Amazon

47224408R00125